PRAISE F(
STRANGE LOOPS

"Gripping. . . . Dense with twists, [*Strange Loops*] builds to a stunning conclusion that somehow feels both inevitable and unexpected."
—Chatelaine

"Smart, sharp, and magnetic. . . . [*Strange Loops*] evolves into a chance to reflect darkly on familial bond . . . and to study the human animal, here so capable and incapable all at once."
—Quill & Quire

"Exquisite and propulsive. . . . [*Strange Loops* is] an unsettling story of doubleness, the messiness and irresolvability of power dynamics, and what it means to be a woman who wants, who desires." *—Kerry Clare, author of Asking for a Friend*

"A slender, wildly compelling novel that asks infinite questions—a dizzying, kaleidoscopic foray into the desires and fears that make us so imperfectly human. I was compelled from beginning to end—this is a novel that sinks into your very bones."
—Amanda Leduc, author of The Centaur's Wife

"Lean and enthralling, *Strange Loops* is brimming with the complexities and questions of human relationships. A story that burns with intensity and daring."
—Iain Reid, author of I'm Thinking of Ending Things and We Spread

STRANGE
LOOPS

STRANGE LOOPS

LOOPS

LIZ HARMER

VINTAGE CANADA

Published by Vintage Canada, a division of Penguin Random House Canada Limited, Toronto, in 2024. Originally published in hardcover by Alfred A. Knopf Canada, a division of Penguin Random House Canada Limited, Toronto, in 2023. Distributed in Canada and the United States of America by Penguin Random House Canada Limited, Toronto.

Vintage Canada and colophon are registered trademarks of Penguin Random House Canada Limited.

www.penguinrandomhouse.ca

Library and Archives Canada Cataloguing in Publication

Title: Strange loops / Liz Harmer.
Names: Harmer, Elizabeth, author.
Description: Previously published: Toronto: Knopf Canada, 2023.
Identifiers: Canadiana 20200278010 | ISBN 9780345811288 (softcover)
Classification: LCC PS8615.A7433 S77 2024 | DDC C813/.6—dc23

Text design by Kate Sinclair
Cover design by Kate Sinclair
Image credits: Narashige Koide / *Naked Body on Sofa* (Naked Female B)

Printed in Canada

2 4 6 8 9 7 5 3 1

Penguin
Random House
VINTAGE CANADA

For Seyward

. . . it is as if desire were nothing but this
hemorrhage. . . . a hunger not to be satisfied,
a gaping love.

    —ROLAND BARTHES,
    A Lover's Discourse

That [Mary Magdalene] is otherwise considered
to be a woman of ill-repute answers to the following
paradox: the "good life" is not a life that conforms to
morals (one can also think of the adulterous woman,
the prodigal son, etc.) but is that which, in this very
life and in this world, keeps itself in close proximity
to what is not of this world . . .

    JEAN-LUC NANCY,
    Noli Me Tangere

The little system contains
the seeds of its own destruction!

    —DOUGLAS HOFSTADTER,
    I Am a Strange Loop

AN OPENING

s'abîmer / to be engulfed

Outburst of annihilation which affects the
amorous subject in despair or fulfillment.

—ROLAND BARTHES, *A Lover's Discourse*

∞

FRANCINE, PRESENT.

The key was still under the clay pot on the concrete front stoop, and that pot made an unpleasant scrape as Francine moved it. The plant inside had long dried and shrunk and was no longer identifiable. But the light over the outer door had flared on when she approached, and the hedges on either side of the walk were trimmed, which meant that her mother had been keeping the place up, regardless of her many threats to sell it or rent it out, to abandon it altogether. On the security pad, Francine keyed in the six digits of her parents' anniversary. Two short beeps chimed, indicating disarmament.

She looked back out into the near-total darkness of the gravel drive. The young man—the boy—was still in the passenger seat, his face illuminated by his phone. She turned again to the task at hand: the inner door's tricky latch and its sticky lock.

"What's up?" the boy said, coming up behind her now. He put his hands on her shoulders supportively. Or perhaps proprietorially. For months he had been trying to touch just these parts of her body—any part of her body—and she had pretended not to notice when he brushed against her, when, overcome by some enthusiasm, he touched her on the arm. Out of long habit she dodged these hands, but then turned around to kiss him. He was so unlike Jamie, who never seemed to want a thing, who, while gentle, had no passion for her, was self-sufficient and lacking in desperation. The boy, though, was tense with desire. He pulled her bottom lip into his mouth; his mouth was soft, was sure. She had spent so much of her life *wanting*. The newness of him was half the pleasure. The other half was how purely and openly he wanted her.

"Come on," she said, pulling him inside the kitchen and towards the cupboards, where she found several dust-filmed bottles of Merlot and, way at the back, half a mickey of peach schnapps. The mickey was fifteen, nearly twenty years old now, purchased by her when she was a teenager—an old transgression that, with time, had lost its charge. She felt now, in all her gestures, a regression: she was moving uncertainly, the way a young woman moves, while this boy was moving like a man, opening cupboards, looking for glasses. When she pulled the cork out of one of the bottles and wine gurgled darkly into one glass and then the other, she couldn't keep her hands from shaking.

"Don't be scared," he said. "I'm not scared."

In the car's dark, the realization that she knew almost nothing about the boy had come crawling over her. The Camry had struggled over gravel roads, had shuddered along dirt ones. He had commented on how little light there was beyond the weak path created by the headlights, and she'd assured him that she knew the way. He talked on and on, and after a while his voice soothed her. He made a future for the two of them out of fantasies that, until a few days ago, he'd been forced to keep to himself.

"I haven't told anyone," he'd said, and named all the friends he might have told, but hadn't.

"Told anyone what?" she'd said, and the words hung there for a moment like the fog from warm breath on a winter's day.

He offered a future. There was so much money. There were cars and houses, resorts and vacations, rooms full of books. The places he'd take her, he said, as if citing the Dr. Seuss book he'd received upon graduating. It was all nonsense. She'd listened to it, already weary, hands on the wheel in the car in the dark.

There were several things she had wanted him not to say, but she hadn't known what these were until he said them. A few times he mentioned his mother, and the word—*mom*—rang out like an accusation, the bell to wake her from a dream. He had tried to talk about the girls at school, how they weren't women, and those words, too, she wished he hadn't said. The word *woman* made her swell and bloat.

Now she quickly downed her wine and poured another glass, keeping her eyes on the boy. They were just several hours down this path and already she'd riddled the whole thing with mistakes. Wrong choice of location, clearly. She hadn't remembered how far away the cottage was. She might have taken some cash and gone to a hotel instead. Of course she didn't want to do this in a car, or in a bathroom, in any public place. But why hadn't she built a fake scenario so Jamie wouldn't be suspicious? Why hadn't she asked the boy if he had any good ideas about where to go? Why not buy him a ticket for some weekend destination and meet him there; why not pretend to go to a conference; why not do this in such a way that Jamie would never know? Why the fuck had she left the way she had—

I just have to get some air.

Don't leave like this, Francie.

I'm going to work, I'll be home in the morning. Don't wait up—

And then the squeal of her tires. Jamie backlit in the door frame as he held their younger son, both bewildered, both sweet. And still in love with her.

THE BOY PICKED up his glass casually, took a neat sip. His pants had cuffs at the ankle, his shoes were what she'd have called moccasins. None of his style choices were familiar to her. He pulled at the bottom of his sweater, that small tug the only indication so far that he was nervous. He was unfazed by the wine, even though he wasn't legally able to buy it himself. He was unfazed by the enormity of the cottage her mother owned, an inheritance from their grandfather, because this boy was a boy of the world, a world where all the people had enormous estates, all the people personally knew famous politicians or actors or somebody. His dark eyes weren't pretty, exactly, but they were penetrating. They contained wit. He was a good-looking, self-assured boy. Not a victim, hardly a boy at all.

She led him out onto the back deck. "We could light a fire," she said. "We could put on some music."

He pulled a small speaker out of his pocket, pressed some icons on his phone, and a low, heavy beat pulsed out. She recognized the song. She had seen him dancing to it once outside the school, had liked the liquid movements of his legs and arms. She hadn't yet felt a desire to touch him, only a desire to watch him move. He had looked up at her, the way he always did, with knowledge and recognition. Who could resist the implication of such a look?

"You can't see it in the dark, but there are cornfields all around us," she said.

"Oh, yeah?"

"There," she said, pointing. She imagined the sound of the fields to be dry and rustling, even though it was barely summer. "And there. When we were little, my twin brother got lost in the corn for a long time. It was really scary. They can kind of swallow you up."

"You have a twin brother," the boy said. "Is he exactly like you?"

"My brother?"

"I want to know everything."

"No, you don't," she said.

"I do." He continued his chatter, told her he'd be going to Paris with his family in a few weeks, and they always flew first class, and the flight attendants never checked his ID, and his parents let him buy cognac, bourbon, whatever he wanted. These revelations of his naïveté were concerning. She wouldn't say the words she suspected he wanted to hear—*don't go on that trip, I don't want you to go*—though she was jealous of his whole future, his whole life, all of the women he would talk to like this.

A silence followed. He lifted her hand and began to move his fingers up and down her fingers, as he had tried to do in the car.

"In the summer, the corn will be taller than you," she said, reminding him of his height instead of his age. She was being careful. She wanted, with him, to be a person without needs. To appear to be such a person. She would resist emotions and indulge only her physical pleasures. With him she would be a man, would maintain the power of a man, would preserve every illusion the boy had about her.

"The last time I was here," she said, "the sky was churning. There were tornadoes touching down all over."

It was five years since she had come to the country house. Despite what Jamie called the family "volatility"—or sometimes

5

"voluble volatility," if he was trying to be cute—her siblings and their spouses had gathered for a weekend under this matriarchal roof to celebrate her mother's sixtieth. It had taken one day to bring the place to a boil. They'd all screamed at each other. In front of babies, at pregnant women, they'd all screamed.

Tonight, as she had walked through the foyer and into the dining room with its darkly glazed hardwood flooring, its Victorian wallpaper in deep reds with small white flowers, past the great room on its southerly side, and now to the back porch, she saw that the feelings from five years ago had, all this time, been here waiting for her. Behind the large French doors, which were bolted open, stood the kitchen island. Five years ago, her mother's slab cake had sat there for a full day and night, pierced with tiny candles like the flags of a conquering country. It had sunk low in the middle, nearly bald of its icing except where it was marked by the trails of children's fingertips, a sandcastle half-toppled by waves. Francine had stood there, hugely pregnant and with her son Simon in her arms, overcome by useless devastation. Simon's real sandcastle had been toppled by waves earlier in the day.

Her mother came to stand beside her, saying primly, "Well, this was a foolish idea."

Her father was not given to shouting. Amid the fighting, and the vomit of one child and the bee-sting of another, Dad had stepped quietly outside and stared at the sky. She had followed him out, Simon in her arms then too, the wind tearing at their clothes and hair, to watch the sky's athletic show. The mid-afternoon world had turned into sudden night. "We'd better get everyone down into the crawlspace," Dad had said. Francine had snorted. These jackals forced into the crawlspace together?

"Why?" Simon said, clutching at her like a wet cat, his fingers digging into the flesh of her arms.

"Because," she said. "Sometimes the roof blows right off the house."

"I'VE NEVER SEEN a tornado before," the boy with the witty eyes said now. Those eyes were focused on her mouth. His desire, the look of his desire, the direction of the look: it was a conjuring trick.

"It was unbelievable," Francine said. Her words, too, were liquefied. They seeped out of her. She picked up her wine glass and took a sip as slowly and attractively as she could manage. Did he really find her beautiful, with these creases everywhere, these laugh lines and frown lines? "That storm was unbelievable because it was too apt. As though our fighting had somehow caused it. Just when we were about to rip each other to shreds, the gods came down."

It was she who had taught the boy *Hamlet*. Who had shown him *Rosencrantz and Guildenstern Are Dead*. And the boy had then asked her about lines he liked—"Give me that man / that is not passion's slave." Had said to her, "Isn't it true that there was a moment for saying no but often you don't know what the moment is until it's past?" He had the admiration of his peers, of girls who watched him as she did. He was a teenage boy who read sonnets for his own pleasure. "Take all my loves, my love," he'd recited to her. And, "Hast thou, the master-mistress of my passion?" And he was a boy who wanted her to listen to the lyrics of certain hip hop songs.

Maybe she was being conned. And maybe she knew it.

"We don't fight much in my family," he said. He lifted his

eyes to hers and held them. He was not the sort of person who needed to ask permission for things. He had stayed after class and held her gaze, reciting sonnets; that was when this thirst had been whetted inside her. "You're my favourite teacher," he'd said then.

She'd told herself then that this was natural. Nothing needed to happen. Attraction roved around and didn't mean a single thing. Or maybe he'd wanted to see if he could seduce her, because, being rich and beautiful, he was bored. Or else this was nothing more than a rush of dopamine, the thing that happened—it was now well documented—when a person held your eyes that way. There were buttons you pushed and the body flooded with chemicals. That was why she could no longer eat or sleep. She consoled herself that Shakespeare and his passions were long dead. She and all the people she knew would one day be dead.

But now, in the moment, half-aware that all this—everything they were doing—was illusory, she clung to the idea of him. His stillness and his newness were a life raft. He would somehow *save* her.

He put his hand on her neck and held it there. They kissed forever that way, until she thought the kissing alone might bring her to climax. It was at that moment he put his fingers on her thin blouse's top button, just that one, and with ease, undid it.

PART ONE

fou / mad

Love drives me *nearly* mad, but I do not
communicate with the supernatural, there is nothing
of the sacred within me; my madness, a mere irrationality,
is dim, even invisible; besides, it is entirely recuperated
by the culture: it frightens no one.

—ROLAND BARTHES, *A Lover's Discourse*

1
—

FRANCINE, HIGH SCHOOL.

When Francine was sixteen, half her lifetime ago, her twin, Philip, became passionately and unexpectedly religious and devout. Their older brother Steven was away getting the liberal arts education their mother would foist on them all, and their parents weren't religious, so it was Francine who followed Philip to his church youth-group meetings, watching at a remove as the other teens there played dodge ball and ate chips and had heartfelt discussions about God. One girl, she noted with disdain, thought it worthwhile to confess to reading the horoscopes in the paper and wondered if God would punish her for this. An acned boy she recognized from the neighbourhood loved to quote famous passages with horrible seriousness: "The Lord is my shepherd; I shall *not* want." After a couple of meetings, Francine had grabbed Philip's Bible and read some of it

with curiosity but no feeling. ("Be wise as serpents and as innocent as doves.")

Philip bruised easily. He told her that he was going to church
partly because he hoped it might be a place free from meanness
or bullying or gossip. Francine was the cynical one. She knew that
there was no such place on this earth.

One day, after Francine had attended a few months of weekly
meetings, Pastor Howard—or Pastor Howie, as he preferred to be
called—interrupted the neighbourhood boy who was speaking.
"I'd like to hear what Francine has to say."

She lifted her head from the Bible on her lap and looked at
him. "I don't have anything to say."

"You're reading so intently," he said.

There were two dozen other kids around her, but she was
unconcerned with them. "I'm just reading this bit here," she said,
putting her finger down. "'Vanity, vanity, everything is vanity.'"

"Oh, Ecclesiastes," Pastor Howie said. "My favourite."

It was like a first taste of cocaine. After that, she wanted only
his attention. She jumped into dodge ball games in case he, with
his large hands, might whip her with one of those rubber balls.
She went to the church early and stayed late; she set up chairs and
swept up crumbs in the kitchen. If he needed someone to drive,
she volunteered. Pastor Howie's Little Helper.

Philip thought she was becoming devout, and he enlisted her
in family arguments, especially with their mother, who main-
tained that belief in God was a form of lunacy.

"Where did we come from? What came before the big bang?"
Philip would ask. He had a few arguments in his quiver, and he
pulled them out nervously at dinnertime.

"The fact that there are unanswerable questions does not make belief in a prophet from two thousand years ago the next best idea!" their mother would say, her hair in a dark chignon, waving her glass of wine. She looked to their father for agreement. Their father would never take a side, only nod placidly and move his eyes the way a painted portrait does, seemingly tracking the observer although nothing else moves.

"More people have been killed because of religion than for any other reason," their mother continued.

"Maybe more people have been killed for the opposite reason," Francine said. "You don't actually have numbers."

"I approve of your skepticism," her mother said. "But not of your desire to join a cult."

But it was not Jesus Francine followed, big-eyed and fever-pitched; it was Pastor Howie. If there was liner around her eyes or mascara in her lashes, if she lost weight, if she learned a little Hebrew: it was all for him.

She was already well acquainted with the way a body could be made to feel. She had long ago graduated from the pressure-pain that rose, burning, from the crotch, when you rubbed a Barbie doll against another Barbie doll to the shuddering outcome of what her fingers could do when she applied them to her arousal. And she was always aroused. Near Pastor Howie, her body not only burned and throbbed but—she thought then—rose on its hackles. She was aware of his electrical current, knew when he was within fifty yards of her, just as she felt the current of her mother's pulse, her mother's scent, the particular register of her mother's alto voice. This current between her and Pastor Howie was a sign, she thought then, just as all things were signs.

The Latin word *religio*, Francine knew, meant binding. And there was a Hebrew word for a woman whose husband refuses a divorce: *agunah*, chained one. There was also a word for the binding done by Abraham to Isaac on the altar. But there was no word for how she felt, no word in English or in Hebrew or in the little bit of French she knew. *Love* was no word. *Lust* so paltry, so common.

A year into this obsession, Francine stayed late at the church one evening. Philip was already outside, in the car, but she made him wait. She crept up the stairs to the church offices and down a darkened hallway, beckoned by the glow of amber light slitting around a door. Pastor Howie stood up from the chair behind his desk when she entered without knocking, and she knew from his face that he understood. He came forward and leaned against the front of the desk. It was a pose of welcome and certainty, she felt then. Only years later would she understand how vulnerable he was.

She came closer; he did not move. "Francine," he said, and offered a hand. That enormous hand, now warm where it touched hers, now surging with electricity, seemed a lion's paw and she its tiny ministrant. "My best little lamb," he said. The words were a thrill and a terror. He allowed her to get closer. So close that one of his jean-clad legs was between her legs. This was a breach; it shocked her. She couldn't believe his daring, or hers. There was a dusty smell in the room, the books, their spinal glue, their oxidizing pages. She wanted to move even closer. She wanted to make of his hard hip a hinge, but she was too young, she needed him to do something, she didn't know what she was supposed to do. Every boy she had messed around with had made the first move. Every blow job and hand job had been requested. She lifted her chin to look up at his face just as he recoiled from her. It took a second before she registered the mad honking of a car's horn—Philip outside blaring the sound—forcing them apart.

For a few weeks after this she held on to the glowing secret of her bliss, the bliss to come, a kind of heaven she would spend in Pastor Howie's arms. It would annihilate everything else. But Pastor Howie was sick for the next two sessions of youth meetings, leaving a pimpled seminarian to lead the rest of the group, poorly, in his stead. By the second week of his absence, Francine felt ill. By the third week, Pastor Howie had returned, but would not look at her. As that evening slipped away from her, the closing hymn sung, the closing prayer spoken, she walked her throbbing body towards him. Still he would not look at her. She stared at the Bible he was holding, thinking how she'd like to yank it from his hands and throw it across the room. Finally he spoke. He asked her to meet him for coffee the following Tuesday. He glanced at her only once, with a look in his eyes that seemed boyish—as sheepish as her own brother's—and left.

Philip had been standing behind her, watching. "You ready to go?" she said.

He didn't need to say anything for her to see her own shame blooming in his face.

THE NEXT TUESDAY, Francine stood for a long time in front of her mirror. She sensed that whatever happened would be the end of it, one way or another. She wished for a word other than *blue balls* for the pressure that had been building in her for a year, pressure that a self-mandated orgasm could only partially and temporarily relieve. This crush had made her question her own beauty, her own power. Her blonde hair was long and wavy in the manner of hippies depicted in movies. She wore no bra under her tight tank top.

In the living room, there was her mother half reading a book open on her lap; and beside her was Philip, who liked masturbating too much, whom she'd caught doing so too many terrible times behind unlocked doors, into depressing containers; and beside him her father—all of them, like cows, watching some dumb medical drama. *You fools, you know-nothing fools.* "I'm going out to see Pastor Howie," she said as she breezed through the foyer and out the door.

In the car, she grew nauseous, heaviness spreading from her waist on down. Kin to dread. He would let her down gently, tell her he pitied her schoolgirl crush, and she'd know that she'd missed her chance in the office that night.

She met him in the place he'd suggested, a Tim Hortons miles from her home, miles from the church. The tables were full of people engrossed in their own sad lives, men who looked up at her as she passed. There was not a single person she recognized, and for a moment she felt as if the world were full of strangers.

Pastor Howie stood waiting, impossibly adult. The skin on his hands was weathered. Around his ears, some of his hair was grey. She could smell a kind of mashed-potato scent on his breath when he ordered for himself and for her. Then they sat at a table, across from one another, each with both hands around a warm cardboard cup. He was no longer afraid to look her in the eye. She imagined him praying for strength before this meeting, and the thought flooded her. "You're more mature than most of these goofs," he'd told her once, affectionately, referring to the rest of the youth group. Sometimes he called her "turkey."

Up close and sitting directly across from him, she could see that his nostrils were enormous. His eyes were globes. His lips were so wide he could easily swallow half of her face if he leaned towards her. She wanted him to. *Swallow me whole. Let me be inside you. I will live there. I will wear your face like a mask.* Much later, when she remembered this moment, she could recall the words she'd imagined more clearly than Pastor Howie's face.

"I wanted to be the one to tell you," he said. "I have some news."

Of course, she thought, there was the matter of his youngish wife. She was pregnant. She had lost control of her body and allowed herself to become pregnant.

Instead she said, "You do?"

"I have received and accepted a call. From a church in Perth."

"Where's that?"

"Four hours east."

"What?" Her hands dropped her partly raised cup, and a burst of coffee splashed onto her arms.

"I'm very sorry to leave St. D's. Particularly to leave you. You're my best little lamb. You've come so far."

Did he not know what he was saying? Maybe he was unable to understand what a girl could feel. What a girl could think. That a girl could have such desire that an event began to form inside her like bad weather. A trap door opened in her gut and she saw, inside, that something raged.

"I'm your best little lamb," she whispered, hoarsely. "You can't leave. I won't let you."

"I've accepted the call already. My hands are tied."

"You can't leave," she repeated. And before she could think, she was on the ledge: "I love you."

He was unsurprised. His pastoring look came over him, gentle and condescending. "What makes you think you love me?" he said.

"I think about you dying on the cross," she said. "And I'm at the foot of the cross and it just breaks my heart."

For a long time, what he said next would make her hate him. Only much later—only now, in fact—did she understand the kindness of it. It had been his attempt to set her free.

"Oh, turkey, you don't love me," he said. "It would break your heart to see anyone dying on the cross."

This, though, was not true. She had performed the thought experiment many times. He was the only one she cared about, the only one she ever would.

She did not lunge at him. She looked down at the cup of coffee, at its brown lid covered in beige droplets.

NOW SHE WAS on the other side of that gulf between her age back then and Pastor Howie's. And it seemed to her as though the two of them had been sitting for all eternity at that pathetic suburban Tim Hortons and were merely taking turns, switching sides of the table in some perverse ballet. She was the age he'd been then, and she had not seen him for many years, and she now knew several things: that he had known his power over her, that he had known his power over everybody, that a crush was easily divined. How intoxicating it was to be the object of adolescent fantasy, and how difficult to resist it. Through college, she'd had guilty sex with several older men, including one professor, because she'd needed, then, to believe that age didn't matter. Men with large forearms, men with long eyelashes, types that conjured Howie. She'd believed, she'd hoped for a long time, that in one of these incarnations they'd both be free to love each other as they were meant to. To slough off the constraints of their bodies in time.

But the thing she understood in this moment, now that the boy was on top of her, demanding that she say his name, was that the difference in their ages was not irrelevant after all. It was crucial.

"Our souls are ageless," she had said to Pastor Howie, despite how platitudes disgusted her. "How can you refuse this?"

"I don't know," he said.

2

PHILIP, FIVE YEARS EARLIER.

When Philip and Francine were children, people liked to laugh about the Bobbsey Twins, the Sweet Valley Twins. Sometimes he and his sister were treated like freaks, like mystics. Can you communicate telepathically? Which is the evil twin? Yes, Francine would say; and, Me, obviously. Look at him, he's such a good boy, she would say, her tone so taunting that Philip would look over at her with wounds for eyes. "They're nothing alike," people said. In high school, teachers waved at them, explaining genetics to the class, what non-identical and fraternal meant, demonstrating that differently gendered twins can, of course, never be identical. One teacher mused about the possibility that gender identity in twins could become confused, spoke of the "soup of hormones."

Yes, they had formed each other. Into adulthood, so that when one person sucked the air out of a room, the other learned to breathe without oxygen. One person developed a capacity with words, and so the other spoke very little. One hurt, the other felt; and back and forth, and back and forth. Philip knew that there was only room for one like this and one like that on each vessel in the sea, and in each womb. Philip knew, also, the story of Jacob and Esau—how Jacob was born after his stronger brother and so became grabby and wily. Fooled both his brother and father out of a blessing not meant for him. Went on to wrestle with some-one who may have been an angel. While Esau plotted to kill him. Esau moved with all the armies of Edom, finally ready to have his revenge, but he was weakened by mercy, mercy for Jacob.

Then came the family gathering at the cottage that day in mid-July. Their mother, Victoria, had made an extravagant meal for her own sixtieth birthday, a kindness that—Philip only real-ized later—no one remarked upon, since she was considered by her three children to be unkind, and in any case she knew all of them, with their thirty-something lives, were too busy to help. *The full catastrophe*, his therapist called his life: spouse, children, career, pets, ambitions, possessions. His wife, Kristal, took pic-tures of the meal and thanked Victoria profusely, chatted to the others about the beautiful weather: a breeze, a blue sky, so calm you'd never believe the storm was coming, but that was a cliché, wasn't it—that the calm came before the storm. But he didn't know then that the storm was coming, only that he was readying himself, preparing for a fight.

He and his sister had already been bickering. Francine complained about the drive, complained about the obligation to bring a dish to share, complained that their mother had recently been sick and would infect them all, complained about her pregnancy, complained about their mother's snobbery, all without perceiving the tension radiating from him. In his gathering anger as he sat there at the outdoor table, Philip feared he might break his china plate as his fork came down upon it. He was going to make Francine hear him for once. He was not going to make Esau's mistake: he would not relent. He was going to stand his ground when she needed him to fall. These would be his metaphors, and she wouldn't suspect a thing until she had walked into him and found that where he'd once been soft, now he'd made himself into a wall, saying, *no more.* Saying, *not forgivable.*

"What?" Francine said. Finally noticing. "Are you mad at me?"

"No," Philip said. "I'm not mad." But he glared at her. They both had big, round eyes inherited from their Dutch-immigrant father, and he saw hers pull wide. "But I do have something to say. Sometimes," he said, "when one person has a lot of force, others can't find their footing. This is why you are responsible for your effect on other people."

The others were looking at him. The short speech had come out of nowhere; he could see that no one understood what he meant. After a pause, Kristal made friendly noises about the food, chatted with the children. Victoria's face clouded and turned mean.

"Philip is making a deep and serious comment," Francine said. "We should all listen up."

"*Straight* to sarcasm," he said.

"Oh, was I being sarcastic?"

"You are not a good person," he said. Held that tension in his fork-gripping hand, held it in his jaw. "Some people aren't any good."

Her husband Jamie looked up, wary. "Let's not do this," he said. Always protecting Francine.

"Are you saying *I'm* not any good? I've sucked up all the villainy and left you pure?"

"Don't put words in my mouth," Philip said, but then he needed to stop, hoped to stop, needed to think through what would come next.

"Someone with such a gift for words shouldn't waste it like this," Victoria said. An old barb she kept handy. A sentence meant to eviscerate them both: Francine was mighty with gifts and charisma but wasted these gifts, was lost; Philip was weak and ungifted. His therapist said that his whole family must like to fight. Must love this.

In the brief silence that followed, the breeze outside, so slight until then, began to pick up.

3

FRANCINE, PRESENT.

Years ago, Francine had said to Pastor Howie, "I'm not any good. I'm not a good person."

"Nobody's any good. We're all just doing our best," he'd said, taking her mildew-blackened soul and, instead of bleaching it clean, trying to show her the mould on his own. He had taught her what a man was, what it was like to be a man, when she was only a girl.

But now, here with the boy, she knew he'd been wrong. She hadn't been doing her best. She was worse than other people, and now this was clear. For example, she had made sure that the boy's driver's licence showed that he was eighteen, as he claimed. For example, she had taken him to this isolated place. She saw these things in herself only after the first orgasm, from which height she had no choice but to fall.

When things had first started with the boy, when she'd begun to realize how she relished the sight of him, and how he seemed to want to put himself in her sightlines, she'd craved information about him. She couldn't do an internet search because she knew such searches incriminate after the fact—and because she knew already that she was on the path of life ruination. But she became specially attuned to information about older women and younger men, about teacher-student relationships, about power dynamics, about predation. When, at a child's birthday party, a friend said offhandedly that younger men thought they could learn something sexually from an older woman, Francine saw, from her own sudden interest, that she was pathetic. Later, at home, she looked unflinchingly at her face in the mirror after Jamie had readied himself for bed. The only other lights still on in the house were Jamie's bedside lamp as he read his biography of James Joyce or Teddy Roosevelt (such details glowed vaguely around the periphery of what she knew she would do) and the boys' night lights—Simon's a projection of many-coloured star shapes and Red's a little green turtle plugged into the wall. She stared at herself in the hard light of the bathroom: the smile lines, the crinkle around the eyes, the frown lines between her brows, what she knew to be, at her jaw, the beginning of jowls. She saw herself clearly and understood that the boy was soaking her in fantasy.

Did the boy want to ruin her life? Was he hoping to fool her, to show her that she was a fool? Or had she groomed him without knowing she was doing it? This was another thing you couldn't ask the internet or even another living soul. The thing she did know now was that Pastor Howie had never been a predator. Everything had just happened to him.

And everything that had happened to her after the boy unbuttoned her top on the back deck now seemed part of a quiet postlude to the main event. The unbuttoning, in retrospect, had been the climax without climax. She must have been drunk, or else out of her mind, because she could hardly remember what had happened. When she tried to return to it in her memory later, she saw the car and the watery path the headlights made, she saw herself leading him inside the house, his trust in her. If she had seen his boyishness at that moment, would she still have plied him with drinks?

After the moment on the back deck, they stumbled into the bedroom. He kept his hand on her hand, a little like a child on a field trip, a very small child, and she looked back at him and stopped. "You want this? You want this?" She meant to pose this as a question, but he did not respond one way or another. "You want this." It wasn't a question; it was an incantation. She took him up to the bed that was her bed whenever the family stayed here; the mattress was bare. The windows rattled, light filtered in from the weak moon, and as he unhooked her bra and then pulled down her pants, pulled down her only nice pair of panties—they slid against her skin—she thought they could strip away the meaning of their ages, their names, the existence of anything outside of this moment, which was not a moment at all, which was outside of time (his mouth on her breasts, his thumbs rubbing her out, his fingers pressing toward her ass). "It's going to storm," she said. But he had stopped talking. Finally, she begged him to fuck her.

He let go of her then. "Say please," he said.

"Please."

"Say my name."

"Please."

"I want you to say my name."

She felt as if she would cry. It was too late to stop. He brought his mouth to her ear, bit her lobe gently, and whispered the command again.

She couldn't. She couldn't. She pushed him off and down, and started to take off his shirt, to unclip his belt, the mattress squeaking and sighing. It was like pushing off a ledge, like jumping into cold water, like telling Pastor Howie that she loved him, like that first moment in her classroom when the boy had suggested something was going on between them—"you're distracting me," he'd said—and she hadn't stopped him from talking. In such moments, you stopped thinking and you jumped.

The window rattled so hard she thought it might shatter. "Alexander," she whispered. "Fuck me, Alexander. Please."

LATER, HE SLEPT innocently on that mattress. He was untroubled, was naked, was perfect in his innocence and his nakedness. Even his penis rested unperturbed against his thigh. She opened his phone to see if he'd recorded anything, fearing even an audio recording, fearing not only what it could do to her life but also what it would do to this love, or whatever this was. She feared knowing, but she had to know. Nothing. She turned on her own phone and read through the messages from Jamie. She thumbed in her reply: *I'm getting a lot done. Will call tomorrow.* She sent this, then wrote another: *I'm sorry.*

While the boy slept she took a shower, washing herself with a sliver of old decorative soap. It was a waxy pink hunk that had once been carved into the shape of a rose or a seashell. Likely a rose. She soaped herself hesitantly, feeling that each of her curves and crevices had become unfamiliar by the boy having touched them and looked at them. By *Alexander* having touched them. The half-moons under her breasts. The rounds of her buttocks, the folds of her vulva, the crack of her ass. It wasn't that she was flawless, it was that he wanted her. It was two, maybe two-thirty a.m. Her arms trembled. She hadn't eaten for many hours. She'd forgotten to bring a towel into the bathroom with her and left wet footprints on the floor as she went into the hallway to retrieve one. These traces of herself she left all through the country house, traces her mother, an emotional bloodhound, would easily sniff out. "I know you," she'd told Francine once, when Francine had denied an early trespass, letting boys watch her do a cartwheel in a skirt. "The reason I am worried is because I *know* you."

How would Francine have reacted if that had been her own daughter? Surely not like that. Surely she would not have blamed a young girl for an act done in total innocence. Maybe she had been dimly aware that the boys' intentions had not been pure, had sensed, as one does in a cartoon—a pinched moustache, hands rubbing together—villainy. It wasn't until she'd been upside down—this, too, had happened cartoonishly, slowly— and her skirt had opened up to reveal her blonde legs, her white panties, and her hairless crotch, that she'd felt exposed. But it was impossible to access her real feelings after her mother had narrowed her eyes and said: I *know* you.

She wrapped the towel around herself and wiped the floor with an old cloth underfoot. She would have to remove all traces. She'd bring the towels home with her; she'd burn them. The condoms so thoughtlessly tossed in the trash bin—they *and* the bin would have to be tossed. She and the boy would have to go into town for garbage bags, to create more traces of their presence here in order to erase them.

Why was there running water in the house? Because her mother was paying the bills, tidying things, still managing this place she called her Albatross. The name was an exaggeration. The house was a burden, maybe, but it was also a boon. Her parents owned two properties outright, while she and Jamie held many varieties of debt. Francine padded down the stairs, towel wrapped around her chest, to check the calendar in the kitchen. It was June, but the calendar on the fridge was open to April, and the corkboard held another calendar entirely, the schedule of summer arrivals. Flooded with adrenaline, she flicked through this second calendar. She licked her finger and pushed a page over. June. Her mother was planning to come in a week's time. The cottage was rented through July. Oh, thank god; she leaned back against the kitchen island.

She felt worse now than ever. What good was sex, what good was the fulfillment of desire? What was the point of these needs, these feelings? She would go home tomorrow, shattered by lack of sleep, and be forced to look into the faces of her kind husband, her good children, and to pretend she was exhausted by her work, which she would never finish anyway.

I haven't told anyone, the boy had said to her only last week.

"Told anyone what?"

She'd run into him unexpectedly, at the university library in town. She frequently saw her other students in line at the Starbucks or hanging around the movie theatre, but she had never seen him in any of those places. For nearly a year she'd nursed this unethical crush, disgusting herself every time she was out in public with the hope that he was just around a corner where she might bump into him. You've done nothing wrong, she said to herself that day. Also: Don't do anything stupid. And: Feelings are just feelings.

"Ms. Nichols," he'd whispered.

She was sitting at a study carrel, surrounded by books, laptop screen facing her, pretending to be a grad student, nothing else. Other Ph.D. candidates in her program had remained unshackled by marriage, children, while she laboured year after year, paying tuition and fees, trying and failing to see her thesis clearly, trying and failing to explain what the scene between Mary Magdalene and the gardener/Lord meant. Why did this scene, Christ touching down in his resurrected glory and saying Mary's name aloud, obsess her and feel every bit as compelling as when she'd first encountered it as a teenager? The scene went like this: Mary visits Christ's body after the crucifixion and finds only an empty tomb. She cries in the garden there, and a gardener asks her why she is crying. They have taken my Lord, she says, and I do not know where they have put him. The gardener simply says, *Mary*. Immediately she knows that the gardener is her Lord. She tries to touch him, and he says: "Do not touch me." He says: "Do not hold on to me."

Francine had first encountered the passage in Pastor Howie's youth group. It had come up again later at university, in her reading of Foucault. It held on to her, the *do not hold on to me*. The *do not touch me*.

The boy loomed over her carrel. A true grad student forgot meals, forgot sleep, startled awake on heaps of books. Francine, too, wanted to become so engrossed in her work she could believe she had no body. So that day she'd worn her ugliest jeans, which bagged at the hips; her hair was a frizzed pile. If the tale between her and the boy was to lose its magic, this was how, she thought.

"Oh," she said. "What are you doing here?"

"I had a plan to find a few books of poetry," he said. Of course he would say that. They had spent the year communicating in code. He pushed a boundary, and she, very carefully, allowed it. There could be nothing said explicitly. He asked her to help him find some work by D. H. Lawrence, and she took him to the stacks. Did he want this book? This one? He was as beautiful as ever: cheekbones and jaw clean-shaven, black hair cut expensively.

And that was when she said, "Told anyone what?"

"I'm serious, Ms. Nichols," he said. "Francine." He began to enumerate the things he had not told anyone. What he wanted to do with her. How much he felt for her. How she might be surprised to know that such a thing had never happened to him before.

Where did he get the courage to say such things? Her temples, she was sure, were visibly pounding. When she briefly looked him in the eyes—he was, fearless, looking into hers—it made her desperate. This, or I'll throw myself out of that window!

"The things I want to do *with* you," he repeated. He was, unlike most men, taller than her. It was nice to feel tiny, as small as a dove, as breakable as a tree branch, a cup in his hands. She hadn't felt like this for so many years. She was nostalgia made flesh. She had to look up at him again, and he put his hands on her shoulders, and she did not fight him off. He moved his hands firmly down her arms. "I want to know everything about you."

She had, months ago, prepared a response to this moment. She meant to remind him of her age, of her position, of her husband, her children, the ruin of many lives. "You think you want this," she said. "But you don't."

"I do want it."

"I'm old."

"You aren't old," he said. "And I'm eighteen, now."

This was when she understood: He had come looking for her. Of course he had. He was smart, and he had bided his time until all obstacles were removed. A child of wealth and permission.

"Nothing will be ruined. I'm graduating in two days. Age is a construct. No one needs to know."

"You read a little poetry," she said. "And you think you ought to follow your heart."

He unclasped her arms, stood back and took this in. "Yes," he said, finally. His skin was smooth and darker than hers. His lips beautiful when they smiled. "I love these things you say, Ms. Nichols. Francine."

"I wish I were your age," she said, as he came closer. No matter how close he got, his face was perfect. He bent his lips to her.

"As it is," she said, "as it is, we can't do this." But already the gap was breached. For a year it had seemed as if it would never be, and for much of that year she had hated him, had hated herself, had hated anyone who got to be near him, and now he was touching her, kissing her, and it was her fault, the fault of her mind.

"What are you doing down here?" Alexander said.

She hadn't heard him moving above her or down the stairs, hadn't seen him approach. He stood between the French doors. So tall, naked, his penis high and hard. His dark hair grew in a T across his chest and in a line down the middle of his torso, lovely as two calligraphic brushstrokes. Maybe he thought this was adulthood. When really it was the sex of young people during their brief respite from a lifetime of rules.

"I had to check on something," she said.

He came near, he put his lips on her neck. "You had a shower."

"Yes."

"This is hot. The towel."

His desire again overpowered her good sense. Perhaps it was because she'd been exposed for a year to the contagion of his hormones. Unbidden, the memory of his last essay came to her. She'd been disappointed to find it mediocre.

He took the towel off her body and placed it on the counter. Then he lifted her onto it, kissing her neck, her nipples, pulling her breast into his mouth. He had taken a condom downstairs with him, and he tore it open.

4
—

FRANCINE, FIVE YEARS EARLIER.

A tornado, a days-long fight.

On the first afternoon of the gathering at the cottage, Francine's family sat around a long outdoor table decorated with blue-and-white striped country linens. There were darker blues and whites on the matching china (Francine's parents never used plastic or paper). On these her mother had placed homemade side dishes. In pottery made by one of her mother's neighbours sat tuna macaroni salad with egg and its tang of relish; sweet, creamy coleslaw; and a salad featuring fennel, beets, and walnuts. Patties of meat for the non-vegetarians had been barbecued and carried over in a glass casserole. Patties of soy and other beans, chunks of kale and quinoa, were crumbling in a separate casserole dish. The spread was beautiful, as if out of a magazine, and doubtless this heightened lifestyle aesthetic was what her mother had intended.

Philip's wife Kristal was taking photos of the children and their chubby hands smeared with mayonnaise, of Celine whispering something in Simon's ear that made his eyes open wide, of the side of the table where the willow swept its long tresses as slowly as an elephant's trunk—or as one imagines the movement of an elephant's trunk. In one photo, Philip brandished his fork like a sword, pointing at someone. Francine, already, was on her guard. In this set of photos—which, in spite of what happened later, Kristal posted online, tagging Francine in half of them—she was scowling. Lines gouging the space between her brows. Glaring, a hand placed defensively on her eight-month pregnancy, the shelf of body that was Red's heel, the heel of the-one-who-would-be-Red.

Victoria was an art history professor. *To the Lighthouse* was her favourite novel. When she lived rustically at her "cottage," she preferred for the cottage to have the appearance, but not the damage, of being sun-bleached or sand-blasted. She was an aesthete; she claimed not to believe in the virtues of deprivation. In the photos that day, she wore white linen pants, a flowing white shirt, and her hair, too, was a shock of white straightened in a severe bob. Silver dangled from her neck and wrists, her slender hands sprouting from bracelets. Her lips were bright with paint. (She called the colour "paint" instead of "makeup," a word she despised.)

Yes, thought Francine: there could be no deprivation, only punishment. No one's eyes were red-rimmed yet, no one's lips were trembling. No one was yet vomiting in an upstairs bathroom, nor being whipped by a sadistic wind, nor going hoarse from screaming. Not quite yet. For now, for the time it took to make these photos, to embed them deep in memory—Victoria would later claim to hardly remember the fight that followed—the images showed a beautiful, educated, witty, happy family. It was Victoria's birthday. She was sixty. She held her gentle husband's hand and looked around like an appraising queen. This was hers.

Later, Francine couldn't pinpoint precisely when the family began to behave like a weather system, each individual a swirl of desires and resentments. Philip had come with his "guns blazing": this was how she put it later to Jamie. He had come ready to fight. And she and Philip had so much power—more, together, than her mother—they were like a gravitational force pulling everything down into it, a black hole.

She did not notice the trap at first. Jamie had been raised by blue-collar people, a steelworker and a secretary, and Francine was often embarrassed on Jamie's behalf by her mother's show of wealth. Sitting over the decadent summer spread that first afternoon, she began to complain. Just who were they pretending to be? Victoria said something about reusable linens and dishes; said something about the way some other people threw things away.

"Not everyone can afford to appear so virtuous," Francine said.

"I don't think that's true," said Victoria. "It's in the end very expensive to buy plastic cups. Expensive in many senses of the word."

Francine blushed to think of her mother-in-law, a woman who stocked her fridge with two-litre plastic jugs of off-brand diet soda, who used saran wrap and threw paper plates filled with food into the trash instead of composting. "Many things look like environmentalism that are really just displays of class solidarity," Francine said. "Wealth is not a warrant. It is not proof of someone's good choices. You think the rich are morally superior," she accused her mother.

"And I suppose you believe the poor are morally superior?" Victoria threw back. "How sentimental. Almost Dickensian."

"Francine doesn't believe anything," Philip said. He stared at her with an open challenge on his face. If he hadn't been her brother, she would have thought he was looking at her the way a daring flirt would. "She's an utter nihilist. No beliefs." This declaration surprised her—she was *full* of passionate beliefs. Philip was the nihilist.

"A nihilist?" she said. "What?" She turned back to her mother. "If it lets you off the hook to call me sentimental for not being classist . . ."

"I don't know why you are provoking a fight. This is a beautiful day," Philip said. "You always provoke a fight."

When she later rifled back through her memories of the day, she couldn't recall what she'd done to trigger the fight. Was it just that she was complaining too much when she was meant to be grateful? That she was growing too left-wing for her bourgeois upbringing, that she wasn't behaving with the poise that would justify her mother's grooming? That her brother was the good boy coming to Victoria's defence? Victoria, with her expensive hair and clothes, her silver jewellery, her well-turned WASPy cool, hardly needed an army. Francine had looked helplessly to her father, whom she always felt would have loved her if her mother hadn't been there every day of his small life. *There* was a man without desires, a man who had once told her that the aspiration of the real epicure was to eliminate as many desires as possible so as to more easily find satisfaction. He was busy cutting up the food on Simon's plate, and would not look at her. A storm was coming, and when she remembered this scene later, Francine imagined that the sky was already darkening with those roiling clouds. What should she have said to quell things? Certainly not the thing she did.

"Thank god for Philip," she said, making a show of sitting back, moving her arms through the air in a sarcastic invitation. "Here with his keen observations to set us all straight."

"Fuck you," he said quietly.

"Philip," Kristal said, putting her hands over Celine's ears. The girl protested, peeling them away and giggling.

When Francine felt anger pulling tight in her arms, she also felt a path forking, understood that there was a moment to choose the other path. In one of Howie's best sermons he'd said, "When God tells us he will not tempt us beyond what we can bear, this is what he means. He's giving you a chance. He always gives you a chance." She did not take that chance.

"Please tell us what we're all like, Philip," she said. She knew he'd been going to therapy, reading self-help books about trauma. She found the wound and pressed it. "One by one," she said. "Please psychoanalyze us."

She watched his face, alert to signs of danger. Her pregnancy made her feel vulnerable—or that she ought to be more careful. Jamie put his arm over her shoulders and squeezed the top of her arm. But she didn't need his warning. She could see what was on Philip's face, see that, although he was struggling to seem neutral, his mouth was pulling tight, his eyes becoming slits: he was hideous with rage. It simmered there, a pot about to boil, heat shimmering under his cheeks and eyes.

There may have been another path for her then, but she refused to see it. As though his rage were a creature that could jump into her body and possess her. It was *his* rage she was feeling, *his* resentment. She looked at her mother, who was, she thought, smiling a little. Later she would accuse Victoria of relishing their mutual spite.

"Okay, Philip, don't be shy," Francine said, even as vomit rose in her throat. "Let's have it."

5

—

PHILIP, HIGH SCHOOL.

Philip was too open. Too open to influence, too eager, too affected by criticism. "You're just too interested in everybody's opinion," Francine said. "Everything shows on your face." A blush, a grimace, a sneer. Even when he felt as if his face had no expression at all, she'd see past that too, and tell him what he was thinking. Expose the wheels turning behind his eyes. The cogs and gears. This was how Philip knew he would never be cool. Francine was an overthinker too, but she was a girl, and also capable of cruelty, and so she would always be cooler than he was.

At sixteen, angst began squeezing him—was this life? Just, this? What was it for?—and then a kid in their class named Jordan became a Christian. He'd been an avowed atheist before, but now Jordan was certain that there was a God. He would try to force teachers into debates and apologetics. Observing him in class, Philip was struck by Jordan's face, lit as though by a halo, eyes fierce and fearless. His face seemed to say that nothing could be more important than this conversation about the meaning of life. *Finally,* Philip thought.

In English class, Jordan would raise his hand with a polite smile and ask what people thought came before the big bang, what people thought happened to their soul when they died— the fundamental mysteries. The English teacher would become exasperated and tell Jordan to write a poem and hand it in for extra credit. In history class, Jordan asked why we humans have such strong moral beliefs if life on earth had only appeared by chance and moral absolutes were therefore unknowable without divine revelation. This prompted the history teacher to give a long speech about the separation of church and state, which devolved into a conversation about state funding of Catholic schools, the fact of which proved there was no separation of church and state. While the history teacher's back was turned, Philip saw one of the other kids throwing his backpack out the first-floor window into a hedge and then climbing out after it, causing an uproar of laughter that the teacher either didn't notice or chose to ignore.

His own questions intensified. What *is* life for? Philip began to think that maybe Jordan knew.

He told Francine about Jordan's line of questioning in class, and she said, "Oh, that's interesting, kind of early existential-ism"—as though she knew anything about existentialism.

"Yeah?" Philip replied, surprised at his sister's positive reaction. They were both sitting in the kitchen doing homework, waiting for a frozen pizza to rise and bubble in the oven. This was after their brother Steven had left for college and Francine and

Philip were largely on their own after school. Their father called them the "Latchkey Twins."

"I don't really know anything about existentialism," Francine conceded. "But I read this one thing by Camus about the idea that—maybe it's Dostoevsky . . . What?"

"What?"

"You're giving me a very . . . skeptical look."

"Is this because of Dre?"

"Is what because of Dre?"

"All this reading?"

Now she was the one who blushed. Dre was in twelfth grade, and a rumour had gone around the school that Francine had *sucked him off*. Francine's coy denials only agitated Philip more. And there had been one party they'd both gone to where she'd ended up in a closet with another older boy.

"I read for my own pleasure," she said. "Anyway, I'm over Dre."

"You shouldn't go after a guy in grade twelve," Philip said.

"I know," said Francine.

Philip had been concerned that Francine would get pregnant and ruin their lives ever since they were thirteen and Francine had started leaving blood-soaked tampons wrapped in toilet paper in the bathroom trash. Steven had told both of them that girls had a different responsibility when it came to sex. *Women have all the power*, he had joked; this was a couple of years before he'd come out. The words had stuck with Philip: girls had a different responsibility when it came to sex because they had to deal with consequences. He remembered their mother's constant refrain about what happened to girls who lacked good boundaries. A man will have sex with anyone, his mother had said.

"Just because a person wants to have sex with you doesn't make you valuable." What, wondered Philip, was *he* supposed to do with this information?

Sucked him off. Philip couldn't get the phrase out of his mind.

It was an autumn day and the sun had already set. The kitchen's unshaded windows and its large glass sliding door to the backyard reflected the image of him and his sister at the table, surrounded by textbooks and binders, their two bodies wrapped in sweaters, jeans, heavy socks. They both loved the intense drama of the season's weather, of cold and rain and wind and forced hunkering.

"Tell me what you know about existentialism," Philip said.

"If there is no God then I should be able to commit murder and face no consequence to my soul," replied Francine. "That's the thought experiment driving *Crime and Punishment.*"

"Did Dre tell you that?"

Francine laughed. "So what if he did?" She got up and went to the stove to check on the pizza, which was still undercooked. The phone's caller ID light blinked red with a message and she peeked at the number on her way back. "Maybe I'm a kind of trickster or huckster or something, like someone who could trade up her wiles or whatever to get knowledge."

"Her wiles? Huckster? What's a huckster?"

"You know, a snake-oil salesman or—like I don't *mean* things the way other people do." He must have looked alarmed by this, because then she said, impatiently, "Stop trying to make me clarify things!"

"So . . . the existentialists defend murder?" What kept everyone from killing each other, anyway? he thought. What keeps us from raping, killing, stealing? If it isn't the Ten Commandments or the threat of prison—what then? And why did he want to be good, want the world to be good?

"Maybe when everyone realized there was no God," Francine said breezily, "they started to wonder about whether moral codes still meant anything."

"How do you know there is no God?" Philip said, startled, but just then the phone rang. It was their father, asking if they'd found the elaborate note he'd left and were feeding themselves.

A FEW DAYS later, Philip approached Jordan in the cafeteria. "Hey, man," Philip said, cringingly aware that every word he spoke sounded awkward and rehearsed. "I was kind of interested in your whole thing about God. Like, what does come before the big bang? Why were there any gases just out in an enormous void? Why is there . . . matter?" Philip felt the concepts wriggle out of his grasp. "You had Mrs. V totally stumped."

Jordan radiated a glow and a shine. Some chemical process had occurred: you figured things out, and then became beautiful. Later, Jordan would explain this using the Bible: You can tell them by their fruit! And, There are no coincidences under heaven. For a week, Philip sought him out during every lunch period to quiz him about the universe until finally Jordan invited Philip to join him at the youth group. He had passed some test.

The night of the youth group meeting, Jordan insisted on driving, even though Philip preferred his own K-car, which he loved like a pet. In Jordan's car, Philip was quiet as Jordan rambled on about his life as a nominally Catholic, functionally secular Filipino Canadian child of divorce. It struck Philip that Jordan talked about Pastor Howie the way Francine used to talk about Dre, who had long black hair that fell into his eyes à la Trent Reznor and had once taken her for an inexplicable drive to nowhere in his car. Francine had asked Philip if he thought that drive was a sign Dre liked her. And did Philip notice the way Dre stopped to look at her when she was at her locker, seemed about to talk, and then turned around and walked away? Did he know that Dre seemed like a badass but was actually very smart, and his favourite book was *Fear and Loathing in Las Vegas*? Had Philip even heard of gonzo journalism?

Now, as Jordan talked about Pastor Howie in the same devoted manner, Philip wished that he had Francine's capacity to fall head over heels for an object of desire. If only he wasn't plagued by these bigger questions. If only he could instead indulge petty concerns over whether one person liked another person.

The church had its churchy accoutrements. A big white cross on the outside and another big, smooth wooden cross inside. Jordan gave him the tour. Wooden pews, long aisle down the middle, all contributing to that hallowed feeling you got in a huge, quiet room with stained glass windows. Jordan took him to the basement, which held a small gym and a kitchen, and then to the carpeted upstairs rec room–looking space, which was where the group went after "blowing off steam" to "get down and dirty with scripture."

"You're going to love Howie," Jordan said.

"Yeah?"

"And Howie is going to *love* you."

There were several dozen kids there that first night, a Thursday. Over the next two years, as word of mouth about Pastor Howie spread, the group would swell to sixty or seventy some nights. If Thursdays weren't enough for you, you could come to church on Sunday, too, and you could go on wilderness retreats or to touch-football games. You could make the church your whole world. That first night, after Philip and the others got sweaty playing dodge ball and then sat in the upstairs space emitting wafts of BO, Howie stood in front of them and lifted them out of the sad limitations of their bodies.

Some of them sat on couches; Philip was next to Jordan on a straight-backed chair.

"Do you ever feel like something's missing?" Howie said. "And nothing can fill it? No matter what you do?"

The questions were rhetorical, but Philip nodded. Howie was broad in his body, a man where the rest of them were still boys. Wide shoulders, thick forearms, a five o'clock shadow on his George Clooney jaw. Downstairs earlier, when Howie had been leaning with his man-body against a painted cinder-block wall and talking to some of the girls, Philip hadn't thought he could be a man who knew anything. But now he heard it. (*He who has ears!*)

"Do you ever feel like everyone is scurrying around and has missed the point? That the world is amazing—that you are amazing—that you are meant for more than this?"

Philip quickly looked over at Jordan, who was also lapping this up. Some of the girls were paying attention, but one girl wearing a short skirt and black lipstick was sitting in a boy's lap, and this felt wrong to Philip, to the point of being evil. Still, no one said anything to her. Howie looked right at Philip. "You were *made* by God," he said. "You were made for more than this. You were made with intention and love. There is a reason"—he looked slowly at each of them, his eyes so intense in meeting theirs it seemed he was reaching out to touch their faces—"you feel this longing." Later, Philip would understand that what he was feeling had a name. The spirit flickered over him; the spirit flapped its dove wings; and Philip closed his eyes and received it. "Hey, do you turkeys want to pray with me? You can ask Jesus to arrive, to enter your own beloved heart."

As though his body were cracking open, as though this were a doctor setting a bone, as though he were falling from a great height—later, when Philip tried to describe how he had felt, Howie told him that some people called Jesus the great physician.

Howie, so large, so compelling: for years afterwards, Philip would wrestle with his feelings about that charisma. Was it merely the spirit embodied in man? The Holy Spirit filling a person as people had been filled on Pentecost? And if you were a good salesman, and knew it, did it matter what your motivations were and what you were selling? It was important, Philip concluded, to be able to persuade people of certain things. You want to persuade children not to be bullies; you want to persuade teenagers to avoid drugs; you want to persuade good citizens to vote. Howie was putting the force of his charisma to good use. His smiling face beamed, and you hoped he'd turn his head and shine that beam on you. Everyone wanted to receive this light, not only Philip. He soon believed that this little community was a taste of the good life Jesus was offering.

In the week after attending the first meeting, he and Jordan met to pore over the Bible together. They lay on the floor of Jordan's bedroom, speaking in reverential tones about what it must have felt like to be an ordinary fisherman and then for Jesus Christ to sweep by and call you to your real life.

"But that is what's happening to us!" Jordan said.

Jordan's mother indulged their earnest conversations, providing them with plates filled with elaborate snacks—cheese and dried apricots—saying how funny it was to see the traditions you yourself had left become deeply attractive to your children. There was no way to escape the cycle of history, Philip heard her say.

Back at home, sitting at the kitchen table, Philip's mother wasn't so indulgent. "How is this not a cult, I'd like to know," she said. "Let us know if they start offering Kool-Aid," his father joked. But Philip was inside a love affair. Of course his parents didn't understand. The spirit of compassion filled him. The spirit of patience. His mother was fundamentally unsatisfied, and he had found the font of satisfaction.

"You seem weirdly happy," Francine said. She said she wanted to see the source of that happiness for herself.

When both parents were home, dinners like this were cozy and warm. Wafting smells of turmeric and garlic. The long walnut table had been built and finished by their father, and their mother set it with antique white napkins and tablecloths she had acquired at flea markets and from her own parents. The possessions of these dead maternal grandparents were everywhere, even extending to the country house, a cottage they had always called "Grandpa's House" and that now would be theirs. Their mother complained about the largeness of her life, the many possessions that owned her instead of the other way around, the time it took to care for things, to keep them from rotting. "Between motherhood, teaching, one's vocation, and one's home, one's homes—I know it is ghastly to complain—there isn't any space in which to breathe," she said. Her oft-mentioned fantasy was of a small one-room apartment with very little furniture. A window, a bed, like an anchorite's hovel.

"Don't expect me to babysit any grandchildren," she warned. "I am not that sort of woman."

"You want to live in a *home*," Francine retorted. "What you're describing is a room in an asylum."

"And so be it," she said. "You're too much like me, Francine, and it worries me."

Francine's eyes flashed in a way Philip could not interpret, although he sensed she wanted to slice through any tether her mother tried to weave. Surely, this was what it meant to sin. To wish to float loose; to wish, in a way, to die.

THE DAY CAME when Philip felt called to come forward and to be anointed, and he asked Howie to meet with him privately, thinking of how Jesus was always getting swarmed by thousands of hungry people, but even when he was exhausted, he made time for them. In his small office, Howie had taken his big thumb and dipped it in oil, and then he had pushed that oiled thumb in a vertical line down Philip's forehead, and then he had swiped a horizontal line to intersect it, and where the oil sat on his skin Philip felt a warm, lingering glow.

"My sister wants to come to group, and I don't think I want her to," Philip told Howie just before they rejoined the rest of the group. The office was lined with bookshelves and piles of books, with ceramic mugs grimy with old coffee on dusty surfaces.

Howie's hands were clutching an under-inflated red rubber ball from an old dodge ball game, and he looked at Philip thoughtfully. "How old is your sister?"

"She's my twin. She's my age."

"And why don't you want her to come?"

"I don't think she's genuinely interested in God," Philip said.

"We cannot know her heart. Only God can know that."

"Yeah, but I'm afraid she will spoil it—afraid she'll tease me or the other kids."

"We can deal with that when it comes to it," Howie said. "They know us by our love, right? And our love makes us untouchable by any evil the devil can bring our way."

"I guess that's true," Philip said.

The first time Francine came with him, she was quiet and gentle. She smiled and spoke when spoken to. He didn't see her roll her eyes even once.

Philip loved the feeling of the church during weeknights in late autumn. A sanctuary from the dark and cold outside; the safety and warmth of being with others within. Jordan had told Philip that one of the girls in the group had a crush on him, and this small piece of news set Philip spinning out a future: maybe he'd find a way to live a real and actual life, to date a girl and get married and go to school and have a job and live all the cozy autumns he wanted until his life came to its natural end.

At one point in the evening, kids were scattered throughout the recreation area, some in corners whispering and giggling, some shooting hoops. Francine was over by the kitchen, eating a ruffled potato chip, and Howie was yanking open a new bag. Philip thought: So what if she wasn't a believer and never would be? Wickedness might find its way in like cold air through a crack, but this place felt warm enough to absorb it. It would absorb Francine, and it would absorb the girl with the black lipstick, and it would absorb the guy whose last name was Leek and who looked grungy—Francine's type—and who sometimes told Philip to *fuck off* for no reason.

When it was time for Bible study, Philip observed Francine reading and taking notes. Later, in the car on the way home, she said how hilarious some of the little passages were. She found something in Jeremiah that seemed like lunacy to her: *Do not let the prophets and diviners among you deceive you. Do not listen to the dreams you encourage them to have.*

"Well," he told her, "you really shouldn't let diviners deceive you."

"Okay," she said. "But what does it mean, 'the dreams you encourage them to have'?"

"Maybe the people were trying to get psychics to tell them stuff, or—" Philip said. "What book did you say that's from? I've mostly been focusing on the gospels."

"I'll grant you that the group is more interesting than I thought it would be," Francine said. "Doesn't seem completely without benefit."

"You sound so much like Mom sometimes."

"Please don't say that."

"You do."

"Take it back!"

They argued until they were both laughing. Francine started to swing her head around, her hair flying and whipping like in a music video. "Would Mom do *this*?" she yelled, opening the window and stretching her torso through it, sticking her tongue out at him. He yanked on her pants, trying to get her to come back into the car and put her seatbelt on. It was a dark night. His tires felt slippery, driving over bunches of wet leaves.

She was screaming and laughing into the night.

"Francine, come on," he said. She had let go of her grip on the car and only her legs were still inside. "Please, God, please," he said, suddenly wanting to sob. There was too much to keep track of. He imagined everything that could go wrong, his eyes on Francine and his eyes on the road, on the traffic signals, other cars, the speedometer. No one could manage all this.

"Hey, it's okay, relax," she said, slipping back in. It was only then, the moment she clicked her seatbelt back on, that he let the car drift into the oncoming lane, swerving out of the way of a truck at the very last minute. He pulled to the side of the road, put his four-ways on, and turned off the car. They were both out of breath. Francine's hair was huge and witchy. They looked at each other. "Oh my god," she said. "We almost died."

"Why did you do that?"

"You're the one who almost killed me!"

He grimaced.

"But we're okay." Now she was laughing again, tears streaming down her face. Here was a near-death experience, and she was as breathless as a child at play. "We're okay, we're okay."

Signals still clicking, he turned the car back on. "Would you please stay in your seat?"

She made a circle above her head like a halo, then pushed her hands together, mimicking prayer. They drove for ten minutes in silence. Then Francine said, suddenly, "I'll grant you that that Howie is an intriguing fellow. Wasn't quite expecting him to be as charming as he was." She said this as though the observation was original to her, as though he, Philip, hadn't understood that from the beginning.

IT TOOK PHILIP far too long to notice what was going on. On a Thursday night many Thursday nights later—the twins were, by then, seventeen, and it was a year at least since his anointing and conversion—Philip sat in his K-car in the church parking lot with the windows down and the keys out.

Guilt of many kinds visited Philip. Even back then—in the late nineties, when climate change was called global warming and explained through drawings of sunlight-arrows pointing down on greenhouses and trying to bounce out but getting trapped—even in those days, Philip felt guilty about waste. He would not add a speck of unnecessary carbon dioxide—or was it carbon monoxide? Carbon, at any rate—he would not add a speck of it into the fragile atmosphere.

Philip also felt guilty about sex, about the aggressiveness of his own hard penis, about the desire to subdue a woman and penetrate her, about his fantasies of such women and the emissions he could, with a little bit of touching, draw out. He felt guilty for taking up space in a world where most people still wanted basic amenities. Sometimes in the shower he prayed for forgiveness for having been born middle-class in North America when so many were suffering. And then on top of that there was the shame of feeling guilty, because what did it accomplish?

And where could you go to disperse the terrible vapour of guilt? Church was an answer. It provided him some solace to know that his guilt was warranted—that he wasn't seeing things, he wasn't deluded, that yes, all of them, all of *us*, were evil. The wages of this guilt? Death. And if you didn't want to die, you pinned your sins to Jesus Christ, as the drama cohort at the youth group demonstrated in a favourite tableau. One person in dangling robes would walk around in cruciform, arms spread, while the other kids feigned screaming and/or spitting as they pinned pieces of paper to the robes, paper with words like *idiot* or *greedy* or *mean* or *hateful* or *spiteful* or—his sister's contribution—*lascivious*. The tableau would end with the onlookers watching as their sins were taken in and absorbed by the Christ character. There was nothing to do with their shame but repent and give thanks. Go and sin no more. It was the only remedy.

Why, Philip wondered, should he have more guilt than Francine, for example, who did whatever she wanted and didn't seem to care what anyone thought of her? The way she openly flirted with Howie, to the point where even Jordan had gently said to him, "Fanny is being a bit slutty." Her behaviour made the other kids uncomfortable, yet now it was she who was staying back for extra Bible lessons when it had once been Philip and Jordan. It was cheating, to go through life without ever thinking of your effect on anyone else. It was *sick* of her to have followed him to the church, to have inserted herself into the youth group—but she *was* sick, so why not? Why wouldn't she? Of course she would.

Meanwhile, Philip had been trying to sin no more. Pastor Howie had been helping him, and under his guidance Philip had tallied his own list of sins to work through methodically. Pastor Howie suggested that Philip try to see if, with all his intentions directed that way, he could go a whole day without sinning. We are always sinning, Pastor Howie said, so just remember that this experiment will fail and only serve to throw you into Christ's awaiting arms. But Philip was undaunted.

He had started his trial one morning the week before, after preparing a notebook wherein he would scrawl his sins. The sun that day had shone into his bedroom, blessing him with light. He brushed his teeth and washed his face, reminding himself to take no pride in his good hygiene. It was a fine line that separated delight from sin. When he showered he avoided going down the mental path that would lead to the pressure that begged for relief—instead, he let cold water pour over him and washed his penis with only as much care as was necessary. If images arose in his mind of the smooth curve of a woman's buttocks, breasts squeezing together, the idea of the sound of a woman taking pleasure, he suppressed them. He squeezed his lips shut and refused. The first twenty minutes of his experiment went smoothly.

He had forgotten about his sister.

That morning, Francine was in the kitchen leaning against the counter and sipping some kind of blended drink through a straw. She was not wearing a bra, and the angles and curves of her body seemed designed to make men sin. Did she mean to have this effect? Most women couldn't help being alluring and the aggressive lust of men was not their fault, but why would you invite it?

"What's that?" he said, trying for neutral cheer.

"What's it look like?"

"It looks like a strawberry milkshake."

"Yeah. I blended some strawberries with milk and ice."

"Can I have some?"

She shrugged. "I guess."

He picked up the glass blender and poured out what remained there into a cup for himself.

"Why do you look all pissed off at me?" she said.

"I'm not."

"Are people messing with you at school again?"

"Shut up," he said.

"I'll set them straight if you want."

"Don't bother," he said.

And just like that, he'd committed numerous small sins of pride, anger, shame.

Now, a week later, he'd been sitting in the car in the church parking lot for way too long, marinating in guilt. He was waiting for Francine to come out while the other kids streamed around the car not looking in at him, not catching his eye or waving or saying goodbye. Howie was the only one who could be counted on to listen to him and to take him seriously. Howie was his sort of man—sensitive to guilt, capable of feeling. He was the only one.

An idea of what was taking Francine so long began to form in his mind, little suspicious breaths inflating a balloon of paranoia. He put his palm on the horn and whaled on it. For a full minute he just held his palm there, crazed.

Francine finally emerged, and he let it go.

"Geez," she said, pulling the passenger door open and sliding in. "What's the hurry?"

"What took you so long?" he said.

"Just let's go."

"What were you doing?"

"Never mind," she said. "I was going to the bathroom."

She was not dishevelled, but the fair skin on her arms was mottled with the red blotches she sometimes got when she was nervous or agitated. Her agitation was a form of electricity. It crackled in the air between them in the car. She was, as their mother liked to say, a live wire.

"Can you just start the car?" she said.

"I can tell you're up to something weird," he said.

"You don't have a clue, you little monster."

He supposed she imagined that she was being affectionate with those words. Later, when they were in their thirties, after years of epic fighting, she would claim she had only ever felt affectionate and protective of him during their childhood. But he'd never felt protected. With her, he felt exposed to danger and to shame.

"Everybody can see what's happening to you," he said. "And I will tell Mom. Because you can pretend to be naive but I know . . ."

"Oh, next you're going to tell me I'm a Jezebel," she said.

He heard the quaver in her voice and realized that he did not want to be cruel. They drove in silence except for the drone of the cassette he had playing, a Christian contemporary mix. When they arrived at the house, she turned to look at him. "Philip, you don't understand. This is not like some big joke to me or something. I'm in *love*," she said.

The quick way she was speaking and her emphasis on that final word made him believe she'd said, instead, "I'm in *pain*."

"Aren't we all," he'd said.

6

FRANCINE, PRESENT.

The next morning, Francine took Alexander to the small grocery in town. Standing in line with him, she realized, gloomily, that she was always in the throes of some crush. Two years ago, it had been her colleague Eli, a history teacher.

"Eli told me I had very expressive eyelids," she had told Maggie, her only friend. "He told me to be careful about my eyes."

"Yeah, I can see it," Maggie said. "His appeal. And everyone knows that about your eyeballs. Don't pretend you don't know."

"But my eye*lids*?" she said. She was into her second dirty martini, and it sloshed, icy, in her glass.

"Get a handle on yourself," Maggie said. "Slow down, young mother of two."

Men her own age were all charm, no character. All ideas, no brain. Eli, this crush, was in his fifties, grizzled and cynical.

Not only did he not believe that he could change a life, but he believed that no person ever changed at all. He drank beer and marked papers half-heartedly. In department meetings he sat next to her and breathed snide comments into her ear.

"I always seem to need a preposterous age difference," Francine said.

Maggie was a little younger than she was, a grad school friend. She was further along in her dissertation, unencumbered by marriage and children.

"Isn't Jamie the same age as you?" Maggie said.

"Yes, well, Jamie," Francine said.

"What does that mean?"

This was a small college town, with too few bars. Francine worried about being overheard. She glanced at the bartender—a white man in tight black clothing with tattoos around his arms—who did not seem to be listening.

"How can an eyelid be expressive?"

"You have gorgeous eyes," Maggie said. The outlandish compliments, Francine thought, women had to pay each other. "And everyone can always tell what you're thinking."

"Right."

"Like right now I can tell you are dismissive of my comment about your expressiveness but also a little worried that it might be true."

"You could tell that from my tone," Francine said.

"Attraction can't be trusted," Maggie said, running a finger around the rim of her margarita, pushing the salt like a bit of snow. "And you aren't in a position to casually sleep with him, just to see."

"People cheat all the time," Francine said.

"Yeah, and their marriages break up and they lose their children. They become disastrous middle-aged people riddled with guilt. They don't have time to dawdle over a useless Ph.D. They end up sending dick pics to the wrong person."

"No one's sending a dick pic," Francine said.

"How would you feel if Jamie slept with someone else?"

"I don't know," Francine said, though secretly the idea of it brought a feeling of relief that slid over her like cool water. "It's not even about sex with Eli, anyway. I don't think about his body at all. It's girlish. I just like being around him."

"Oh, now, see, that's a real problem," Maggie said. "Sex we can deal with. Desire we can sublimate. But, like, imagine standing in line with him at a grocery store. I mean, do you want to spend actual daily life with him? Does that appeal to you?"

"That's the main part of my fantasy."

"Standing in line with him at the grocery store is your fantasy?" Maggie chortled. "Oh, God. Is this what I have to look forward to? Mother of two at age thirty-three. Do you also want to fold his laundry? You want to meet up with him around the kitchen island, butter bread?"

"You little bitch," Francine said, laughing. "I'm not a very good teacher, and the school is really stressing me out, so I'll be happy to leave as soon as I sort out this Eli situation."

"You're staying just because of Eli."

"I guess I am trying to have a career," she said, making airquotes. "And these kids are just out of control. And I still feel like a kid—I have no interest in controlling them! One of the girls asked me if it made me feel gross, the way the boys were flirting with me. It was awful. One of them asked me if I wanted a sugar baby or something."

"This is how rich kids behave, I guess?" Maggie said.

"I guess."

"Aren't your parents rich?"

"Not like this."

Maggie made a face: skeptical, teasing.

Two men at the other end of the bar were staring at them now. It was because of Maggie, Francine was sure. Maggie was buxom and generously hipped, the shape of a fertility goddess. She was wearing a very tight, low-cut pink shirt so that a dark shadow caved between her breasts, and her small roll of belly fat sat below them, an alluring signal of fertility. Francine herself sometimes had the urge to bury her face between those breasts, and she had rarely lusted after women. Soon these twenty-somethings would walk over to flirt, during which routine Francine would fantasize about Eli. He would have shared her cynicism. They were in a bar, and this is what people did, driven by the algorithms of their desires. What was the point of an affair at her age? Francine knew exactly where it was headed. She believed in love: that was the problem. All love is doomed, or it destroys you, or it fades. The best you could hope for was someone to say wry things to you under his breath as you waited in line to pay for your organic fruits and vegetables.

NOW, TWO YEARS had passed. The flame she had carried for Eli was not only extinguished but barely remembered. She could not resist doing an accounting of the time between, over and over, little licks of a whip to wound her. Two years ago, as she'd been flirting at that bar, Alexander had been finishing his sophomore year. Sixteen years old. And before that he'd been a child. She'd been an adult for most of his childhood. She'd been smoking cigarettes and attempting to destroy herself for love of Howie while Alexander's mother had carried him around the room singing him lullabies. He was closer in age to her children than he was to her. These were the facts. There was nothing to be done.

As she and Alexander waited in line, she remembered Maggie's distinction between a harmless crush and a real love affair. The difference was this: wanting to have Alexander with her for everything, the way as a child her twin had been always with her. Philip had once been her best pal, the flesh that was of her flesh, and now she wanted from Alexander not only the thrill of attraction and lust, but also to always have the threat of his body near hers.

Alexander was examining strawberries in their small green cartons. The smell of the berries was strong and sweet. She watched him pick them up and hold them to his nose. His slick dark pompadour had softened overnight, and hair fell onto his forehead. He had said that he was falling in love with her, and the feeling of first love, she knew, was a mania of the senses. You wanted to dwell on each one of them, on each sweet-smelling strawberry, on its vivid red hue. Was it the red of a fire engine? Of a tomato? Or was it blue-ish red; was it, even, purple? Look at its sweet little seeds.

This errand was meant to be a simple retrieval of necessities—garbage bags and wet wipes to erase their presence from the house. The towel she would ball up and take home with her. He hadn't brought anything to shave with, and his face was shadowed with the start of his beard. She had never been with someone so good-looking before. It was an education in beauty. Before this she had mainly been attracted to minds and to ideas of futures and lives. She wanted just to look at this boy, wanted to proclaim his superiority to the world. She wanted to write a poem, to paint a painting, to find some way to pull the feeling of his beauty out of her mind, to exorcise it.

Francine placed her items on the counter. The store had chosen not to upgrade to a conveyor belt and a digital register in order to seem quaint, she suspected. She hated the affectations of this small town. Alexander added to her items the strawberries, a loaf of sourdough bread, artisanal butter, a disposable razor and shave cream. "I thought we could have a picnic," he said.

They were playing house now. Maybe they'd never have to leave.

"That sounds lovely," she said, and she kissed him on his lips. His facial hair scraped her cheek. They kissed for too long, too wetly, and when she pulled away the cashier was looking at them with assessing eyes. The woman was older than Francine, but only just, and had let her greys go natural, waves streaked with white. She wasn't wearing a wedding ring.

"You need bags? That'll be $36.10."

"We do, thanks," Francine said. Let her judge me. Who even gives a fuck? For a brief moment she wished Jamie were there, or even Eli—the men in whose calm cynicism she found shelter.

Alexander had sensed the woman's judgment and responded by putting his hand on the small of Francine's back while she pulled cash out of her wallet. There could be no record of her whereabouts on a receipt or a bank statement, and so when the woman handed her the receipt with her ninety cents in change Francine stared at it regally and turned to leave without taking it.

In the strip of parking spots outside of the grocery, they loaded their items into the trunk of the Camry. It wasn't as though she had killed somebody, it wasn't as though anyone would comb through her car looking for DNA evidence. So what if Jamie found a strawberry that had rolled out of the bag and gotten stuck in a crevice to rot? It was nothing. A child could have done it.

"I have never cheated on my husband before," she said to Alexander. "I've never cheated on anybody." She was adopting the lover's language of self-definition and confession. He pushed her gently against the car and kissed her again. When they pulled away from each other, she returned to her own side of the car. Just as she was about to climb into the driver's seat, she heard someone shouting.

"Fanny? Fanny? Is that you?"

A woman's voice. The town was populated almost exclusively by cottagers and landlords. She knew no one here. And nobody had called her Fanny for more than twenty years. Goddamn her mother for nicknaming her Fanny like something out of the nineteenth century.

"Fanny!"

The woman was upon them. She was roughly Francine's own age, and she came over to the Camry with a large shaggy dog on a loosely held leash.

"Oh my god," Francine said. "Sherri."

"I go by Sheryl now," the woman said. "But yes."

"I go by Francine."

"Ugh. We're so old. Adulthood, right?" Sheryl was wearing a baseball cap over short hair.

"I guess we are," Francine said, thinking how funny it was that women in their thirties are still unable to believe they are adults, even though some had been so for nearly two decades.

"This is Rufus," Sheryl said.

Francine looked down at the dog. "Do you live around here?"

"You know what, I do. Been living in town for the last three years. I teach grades three and four and sometimes two at the elementary school. Just me and Rufus. Nice and quiet."

"That does sound nice," Francine said. "Everyone's a teacher, I guess."

"What are you doing out here?"

"Well." Did she need to lie or was it better to tell the truth? "My mother—my parents have a country house out here. We used to come out when we were kids."

"How's Philip?"

"Fine."

"You're married?"

"What?"

"You're wearing a ring."

Francine looked at her hand.

"Hi," Sheryl said, leaning towards the car and waving at Alexander. "Wow," she whispered. "He's really cute."

"Thanks," Francine said. She moved back behind the open door. "I've gotta go. We should have coffee sometime and catch up. But I—"

"Are you on Facebook? I'll add you." Already Sheryl was taking out her phone.

"Sure, okay. Add me." She shifted into the driver's seat, closed the door, waved and turned the key without looking at Alexander.

"You're all out of breath," he said.

She pushed too hard on the gas pedal, reversed wildly before looking behind her, and then sped down the rural road back to the house. Windows open, hair flying, she felt the same panicked excitement as she had that night of her mother's birthday when it seemed a tornado might touch down on their property. She wanted to race away from this person from her past and return to the cocoon with Alexander. In marriage you proclaimed your love in front of others, but with passion you wanted it all to yourself.

She parked the car outside the house and saw that there was a notification on her phone. Sheryl Macguire wanted to be friends. She ignored this and logged out of Facebook. As Alexander thumped the car's trunk closed, the phone vibrated again, this time with an incoming call. She pressed the phone to her ear and walked down the drive away from him.

"Plan on coming home any time soon?" Jamie said.

"Yes, yes," she said. "Soon. A couple of hours. I'm so stressed, Jay. I'm just not at my best. I forgot to eat. Are the boys okay?"

"Red missed you last night."

"Oh."

"You want to say hello to them?"

"Okay," she said. Her sons gave her news of what they had and hadn't been allowed to do, of what mischief they had caused.

"It sounds windy at the library," Jamie said, when he took the phone again. He said it without a trace of suspicion.

"Oh, I've taken a break. I went out for a walk."

"You can't really do this, Francie. You know I want to support you, but this is way too much."

"I know, I know."

"You slept in the library?"

"I'm sorry," she said, dodging the question. "It's a one-time thing. It won't happen again."

"It's not—will you please go to the café? We'll meet you there and have lunch."

Shit. "No, I can't. I'll be home in a few hours," she said. "I know it's not fair."

Pacing, she had ended up way across the yard, by the willow tree with its nearby meagre stream. Alexander had taken the groceries in and was standing on the back deck.

"I just need to get a few more things done," Francine said. She was acutely aware of how she loved and needed Jamie. He had once been the object of her desperate passion, and she knew she was now living out a cliché about marriage and the death of desire. She loved and needed Jamie—but why didn't he see what she was doing? Why was he not suspicious at all? "I'll be home before dinner."

She was not entirely out of her mind. She could make plans and keep them. She silenced the phone, double-checked that the location tracking was off. Alexander walked over to where she stood by the willow, carrying a blanket, another bottle of wine, and the strawberries. He flattened the blanket and she lay down on it. He opened her shirt and unhooked her bra.

"Don't go to Paris," she said.

"Okay."

"Let's stay here forever instead."

He assented to this too.

"WHEN I WAS a young girl, when I was your age," she told him afterwards, as they picked at the strawberries and tossed their caps into the stream, "I had an affair with an older man, a married man."

"I wish I had known you then," he said.

"That's how I used to feel about him. I wished I'd known him when he was young."

They stood and folded the blanket together. They carried everything they had brought with them to the car's trunk and sealed it within. She went through the house, twice, making sure that water wasn't running and that lights weren't on and that windows were firmly latched shut. Alexander waited for her in the car. Guilt had already begun to burgeon in her, like tree buds. She tapped her parents' anniversary into the security keypad. She locked the door and returned the key to its place under the pot, which once again made its unpleasant scraping sound. Without lifting her eyes to the house again, she hurried to the car, feeling haunted. Now she knew what it must have felt like to be him, to be Howie. Alexander, unburdened, beloved, rambled on from the passenger seat as she pulled down the corn-bordered drive, and the sound filled her with dread.

7

FRANCINE, HIGH SCHOOL.

"Our souls are ageless," Francine had said to Pastor Howie, even as she cringed at her own cheesy platitude. "How can you refuse this?"

"I don't know," he said.

Neither of them made any move to leave. They sipped their way through their short cardboard cups of coffee. She let his words stand, let them ring out, and she began to hate him. *I don't know.* He wasn't going to take what he desired, even when it was being offered to him.

"I hope you'll come to visit me. Bring your brother, too. I'm going to miss Philip," he said, finally. "The church there could use some vitality, some youth."

I hope you'll come to visit me. She considered this sentence, each word of it a sign.

"What is it? Some kind of stone parish or something?" she said.

"I hope someday you'll come to visit me," he said, again. His repetition felt like an attempt to fend off the reality—even the vitality—of her, sitting there. Or that's how she would remember it later: sitting at that Tim Hortons was her origin story, the opening of her own perverse ballet. She told herself, then, that it was time. Time to lean across the table and kiss his mashed-potato mouth. But at that moment, Howie stood up, and after a brief pause so did she. She followed him out to his car and before he could climb inside, she pushed herself towards him, trapping him between her body and the driver's-side door.

"At least tell me that you want this," she said. "Tell me the truth, at least. I need to know." Anger was mixing with her desire; it was baking inside her.

"Francine," he said.

She moved closer. "Tell me that you're moving because of me. Because you love me too."

"Your life is not a Shakespearean tragedy. Your life is not a romance novel. It doesn't need to be," he said. She saw the fear in his face. He seemed about to admit it: that her desire had the force of high winds and had blown him away. He would try to shelter in farm country, five hours away. His face seemed to say what her brother, years later, would accuse her of. That she was not destroyed but destroyer. That she destroyed all things in her path. But she had wanted Pastor Howie to save her and to take her away. She wanted *him* to be ruined, for her sake.

"What is life worth, then," she said, "if it isn't a romance or a tragedy?"

He put a giant hand on her shoulder and gave her a sad look. "You are very important to me. When you're older you'll understand," he said. "Go home."

She shook her head. "You love me too."

"Go home."

She backed away and got into her parents' car, crying so hard that she could hardly see the road. She followed him for a while and then she turned off, rounding back to her house where she cried in the garage some more. Philip and her parents were still watching TV. They stopped to look at her as she came in and she could not look back at them. Her eyes were scorched red.

"Francine?" her mother called from outside the bedroom door. "Francine? What did you do?"

8

FRANCINE, PRESENT.

Francine cut cucumbers and carrots into coins and portioned sandwiches into fingers. When she spoke, she attempted to be calm, but still she worried that her boys, that Jamie could read the language of her pose. Her hand on the knife chopped too hard, and she muttered under her breath. Jamie held Red in his arms, who rubbed his eyes with fists, a babyish gesture. "Mommy, I don't want to go to school."

"I know, baby, I know," she said. "But you have to go anyway."

Jamie sat Red down at the table. "Cereal or toast?" he said. He and Francine had the habits of liberal, overeducated, middle-class parents. They gave their children options, even while they suspected that many options were a road to unhappiness.

"I'll get that," Francine told Jamie without turning around. "It's okay."

"Don't you need to get going?"

"Jasper's opening. I have a few minutes."

"If you stay home for a few extra minutes this morning, you come home an hour too late this evening," she said.

Jamie said nothing, and instead poured Red's milk. Red was Francine's nickname for Riddley, whom they'd named after a character in a book.

"Although I guess it doesn't matter either way," she added.

"Right," he said. "I'll try not to be home too late." He was generally unmoved by Francine's constant stirrings of emotion, and they both agreed this was the reason for their easy marriage. No fight would happen now; none would happen later. *I know it's hard for you to be home all day with the kids,* he'd say, and she'd tell him *she knew he knew and it was just that life could be so hard!* Now, Jamie took his leather bag and kissed them, son and then wife, on the cheek before shouting up the stairs, "Simon! Get out of bed!"

Francine sipped at her dose of lemon water, which she would finish before allowing herself coffee. Long before Jamie, after Howie, she had for a time tried to live with the austerity of a saint. It had been easier, then, to allow herself no luxury. The walls in her old apartment had been mostly bare, only a poem by Yeats pinned up in one corner, lines underlined: "The best lack all conviction, while the worst / are full of passionate intensity. // Surely some revelation is at hand." A single armchair, a set of books. But now she had a house, which she and Jamie had bought together. After a few years of living in it, she'd torn up the beige carpeting from the hardwood, which was itself in ill repair. A few greenish-brown shingles had loosened and slid off the roof. A tree's trunk was wedged into the wooden backyard fencing. There were pipes to keep clear.

But, she often reminded herself in the morning, drinking her lemon water, a house was not only walls and roof, flooring and paint. Behind drywall was the webbing of wood, many screws and other joiners, circuitry and wires and the twists of plumbing. There were appliances and lights, all of them drawing on this system or expelling into it. Everything rusted and wore down. Oxygen and water, these things that kept people alive, were at the same time destroying all that they had. Everything would be eaten up, ravaged. All built things were part of a system designed to fend off decay, but decay wormed its way into everything.

She had been the one to decorate the coffee shop she and Jamie owned. She had thrown a look together that was thoughtfully haphazard, as though the decor had more important things to worry about than whether the chairs matched. The result was appealingly eclectic: a turquoise Formica table, a table with inlaid tiles, a long farmhouse table at the back where the students liked to install themselves and sit for hours. Everything had been acquired second-hand. Francine had driven from thrift store to thrift store in their rented van, had called people she'd found on Craigslist and talked them down. Together, she and Jamie sanded and refinished each piece. It had been her idea to have the board games and chess sets on a shelf, and to have toys available for children. One of their first baristas, who'd since left them for law school on the West Coast, had developed gluten-free and vegan versions of their popular savoury muffins and scones. Now they were the most popular café in a neighbourhood with too many cafés.

But, Francine thought, what was true for the home was true for the coffee shop. Constant effort to keep money and water flowing, with decay the only possible result. Sometimes it seemed to her that every human being was like a house built on a cliff, insisting that the earth below could hold its weight.

She watched Jamie through the front door of their home. He cut prettily along the sidewalk toward the café, his waist and hips in a neat and narrow shape beneath his wide shoulders. Sometimes he liked to reminisce about her old apartment, which was where she'd lived when they first met. She'd thought she'd always live that way. He brought it up sometimes and wished for it, and she knew he was wishing for a former version of her. Once he said, "I kind of miss when you believed in God."

"I never believed in God."

"You believed in God when we met," he said. "I remember you telling me about it. I even told my friends I had met a Christian girl."

She'd laughed at this, but he was dismayed, as if discovering a crucial fact he'd got wrong. Had it really been so important to him that she'd once been capable of belief?

"It was my brother who believed in God," she said. "I just went along for the ride."

Though of course, Francine had never just gone along for any ride.

AFTER DROPPING OFF the boys at school, Francine went to the café, coming in through the back entrance and past Jamie's office where his jacket and bag were heaped on his wooden chair. Footsteps and laughter reached her through the wall from the main part of the shop and the counter where Jamie took orders. It was October, the season of Pumpkin Spice. The café's manager Jasper and a new barista named Willow greeted her with their usual customer-service script—*hiiii welcome*—as she came to the register. A ceiling fan whirred overhead. Outside it was cool, but near the steamers and ovens everyone was always in a sweat. Jamie nodded at her and offered pleasantries—how was drop-off?—distractedly handing her the usual mug of black coffee, which she took to a table against the wall.

She was wearing tight jeans and a beige trench; over her still-new haircut she'd pulled a cloche-style felt hat. Back in late August, she'd cut it short, her Lady Godiva hair, her great vanity. It was naturally dark blonde, and the few silver hairs beginning to sprout were still vastly outnumbered. From the time she'd been a teenager she had always worn it long and wavy, elaborately braided or down. The day when she'd cut it, she had called Jamie from the salon, in tears. What had she done? But by the time she'd driven home, her head feeling small atop a body suddenly revealed as lithe and boyish, as though her long hair had been a disguise, she was over it. "You're shocked," she said, as Jamie marvelled at her.

He laughed. "It looks great. You look great." Of course he would say that. She did not deserve a kind word from him, did not deserve to rely on his sturdy gentleness, but it was freely offered to her anyway. Just like Jesus was supposed to do.

"Now I'm all face," she said. "But who cares. I'm tired of looking good."

After that, she had changed other things, too. She would not go back to teaching; she was taking a leave from her Ph.D.; she wanted to be a mother and that was all. She and Jamie would save on child care and the expense of a second vehicle, and she could plan meals instead of sighing in front of the fridge every night and serving cheese sandwiches. She could devote herself to the café, too. "Safer to bet on you," she told Jamie, in answer to his concerns, flattering him and touching him until he accepted that she'd made up her mind.

Jasper was playing Radiohead over the café's speakers—music from her own youth that was now, she realized, decades old. When she was in high school, kids in the youth group used to play covers of "Karma Police," of "Wonderwall." Now, in the café, the students on their laptops with cords dangling blocked out the ambient noise of her adolescence with earbuds and headphones. A group of three moms sat on the second-hand couches with their toddlers and babies, who played with knitted finger-puppets and miniature John Deere tractors.

Outside, the temperature was crisp as a fresh apple, the light golden. Each autumn brought nostalgia, which was then dutifully harnessed to commerce. Francine had spent the past month hoping to run into Alexander in the village, haunted by lookalikes, other men with similarly dark hair and eyes and sweet cheekbone structure. She'd tried to turn her mind to other topics, but other topics had no force. A future with him would never be possible, was never going to come, but still she remained distracted, could not focus on her dissertation anymore, could hardly read a thing. Her mind was a bird flitting at the slightest possibility of seeing him. Even the hope of this was a manifestation of the disease itself. She could not fly. If she were a bird, she'd be flightless, moulting. Rooted to the ground, she dissembled, she disassembled herself like the trees shed leaves. Parts of her had died and sloughed off, and she did not know how to return them to her body.

It had been six weeks since she'd seen him. He was doing a year at Queen's University with the ambition—his parents' ambition—of transferring to Oxford in England or to Columbia in New York. They wanted him to go to the London School of Economics after that. He had not done as well as he should have in his senior year, he had told her, a hand cupping her breast, because he'd been too *distracted* all year. She winced now to think of it.

When she made her decision to stop teaching, a month ago, she'd offered various explanations. *It's important for the boys and for Jamie that I just stay home for a few years. We're too busy.* She'd given variations on this phrasing several times: to her boss, to her colleagues, to her friends at barbeques and parties, to the ladies on the Home & School committee, many of whom had themselves made that same tough decision. Their husbands were lawyers and engineers and doctors and worked in IT. Now, with her mom-cut—far less flattering than her long curls had been, perhaps—and her tireless volunteering while surrounded by other people with ovaries, she understood that this new passion for organizing children's lunches into bento boxes was a form of camouflage. You pretended to be something until it was real.

She got up to put her trench on a hook near the front door of the café. The fan stirred the butter and coffee aromas. It was the smell of this time in her and Jamie's lives, Francine thought. It wound through their hair and remained on their skin; it would seep into the fibres of their clothing and could no longer be washed out. She tied on an apron and told Jamie he might as well go work on the accounting in the back office. The morning rush was over; she was caught up with housework; if she went home she would only decadently throw herself onto the sofa, read books and fill herself with yearning. Her dramatic streak would swell if not tamped down.

"Are you sure?"

"For an hour, anyway," she said.

Jasper was flirting with Willow, as he always did. Willow teased Jasper about his hair; Jasper fiddled with his lip ring.

There weren't many customers, and there wouldn't be until the lunch rush, with its frantic pressing of paninis and ladling of chili into bowls. The moms sitting on the couches were ones Francine knew from the neighbourhood; Simon had been on an awkward playdate with one of the kids, years ago, and Francine recognized the other women as members of the Home & School. She smiled and asked how they were; they smiled and asked how she was. *Oh, you know.* She did know. She wet a cloth with spritzes from a spray bottle and went around to the few empty tables, wiping off circles of coffee and crumbs.

The summer affair with Alexander had not fixed the problem of her longing; it had only made the world seem more unreal. Her marriage—her and Jamie's belief in their shared home—had been a delicate but crucial weight that gave her meaning. She had always been prone to anarchic cynicism, a sense that words did not correspond to reality but were only a net to cover over the void—the meaningless nothing—that lay beneath reality's sensory grid. So now she dissembled while her leaves sloughed off. But why couldn't she let the real relationships in her life— her husband, her children—ground her? She thought about that phrase—"being grounded"—as she scrubbed at a stubborn stick of dried milk on her favourite turquoise Formica, and how the people who talked about "being grounded" themselves were never actually in need of much grounding. Grounding like an airplane that has been aloft and makes a safe landing? Or like a dangerous electric current? As her brother said of her: a live wire.

She looked up, a scowl on her face, to see Alexander just outside the café's front window.

The moisture from the baking and steaming had produced a white condensation on the glass. In a high-collared black coat, framed by the frosted glass, he looked like a Victorian hero. He walked in and she suppressed the urge to run to him. He sat at a table near the window, conspicuous for not having ordered anything, for not having any computer or book with him. He sat there with his dark eyes behind new, stylish glasses, and she felt him watching her.

"Hi, Ms. Nichols," he said, when she finally approached his table. She dropped the cloth on the table's smooth surface. "How was your summer?"

"Lovely, Alexander, thank you. How was yours?"

"It was all right."

He grinned his smooth-lipped handsome grin. "I like the apron on you," he said.

Through the open door to the back room, Francine could see Jamie sitting at the computer with his numbers and his blinking cursor. His face was bent close to the screen. The baristas fiddled with the speakers, laughed about each other's musical tastes. Alexander had his eyes on her, but no one had noticed. The moms discussed breastfeeding, midwifery, the pros and cons of staying at home. *No sleep, there's never any sleep*—their phrases drifted up and she wanted to catch at them, not as though they were floating, but as if she were, as though these words were an anchor. Students at the long table near the back tapped keys. Jasper twisted his lip ring.

"You aren't in Kingston," she said.

"I'm transferring here," he said.

Love made a person selfish. It made a person helpless to the demands of the self, to the self's gratification. She touched her fingers on the Formica, the tip of each coolly sensing that the world still had substance. The moms, the employees, her husband: they were all abstractions.

"You are?"

"I already have," Alexander said. He seemed to sense that she was about to burst into tears. "I thought maybe I'd see you on campus," he said.

She shook her head. "I dropped out of school." Tried to grab at that stupid phrase, an excuse to make the decision logical: *no sleep, never any sleep*. Instead she said, "Can I get you a coffee?"

He asked for espresso, long. So, he had picked up European habits. She went around the counter and prepared the drink for him, and after she handed it to him in the small cup, she untied the apron, put on her coat and hat, and walked out of the café. He followed her.

"Are you heading to the campus now?" she asked.

"Yes."

"Can I walk with you?"

"Yes."

There would be former colleagues and students around; she affected a pose of mentor to attentive student. Surely no one would suspect a woman who had shorn off all her hair.

"I like your hat," he said.

"Thanks."

"You look elegant. French."

He would have to make every overture. She remembered now how she had done this same thing to Howie, the same thing Alexander was doing to her. Yes, an adult could be turned into a child, helpless.

"How was Paris?" she said.

"Oh, it was Paris," he said. "Paris was Paris, Berlin was Berlin."

"I don't doubt it."

"This pretence is really terrible," he said. "I wish you could have come with us." They walked along the tree-lined thorough-fare connecting village to campus. The leaves: orange, tawny, brown, yellow. Their colours hovered in the air like seconds. They vanished underfoot.

"I don't want to have to pretend anything." As he said this, he slipped a hand behind her coat and around her waist. She allowed him to do this. Her heart beat at a painful speed, as it did when, running, she faced a sudden incline. She endured this as she had endured that. His hand on the small of her back as her hips pivoted left right left right. The ache at her crotch.

"I'm so relieved," she said.

"You are?"

"I missed you."

He pulled his hand away. "I have my own place," he said. "Come see me. Come on Friday morning as soon as you can."

She kept walking alongside him, her silence an agreement to these terms. This love affair was like all love affairs. She was as common as a tree. It would flare up and recede, flare up and recede, and for all this drama nothing whatsoever would change. It would hardly leave a trace.

At the library, he pulled her into a corridor and kissed her, ran his hand over her ass, and then left her for a lecture on the Iliad, for which he was late. "I love Homer, don't you?" he said as he walked away. She leaned back against the exposed brick under the flash of a red exit sign to catch her breath, then went to the bathroom. Her face in the mirror was still a shock. She missed her long hair just as she sometimes missed the babyhood of her sons; just as, in this moment, she missed her steady husband in the back room with the spreadsheets. After drying her hands, she walked home, listless and aroused, vaguely unsettled. She was struck by an odd thought: a sense that her brother had seen her with Alexander. Sometimes Philip was unpredictable, would show up at the coffee shop with a sanctimonious look on his face and order a sixteen-ounce cup of the fair-trade drip, as though he and Francine hadn't been feuding for five years. They weren't in touch by phone or by text; he never returned her sporadically blurted attempts to connect that way, nor by email, nor even, anymore, through her parents, who had acted as mediators and messengers for a while.

Her mother had been part of the problem, part of why the attempt to connect had failed. She was a complicated messenger—she seemed to abhor femininity, and also Francine, but claimed to be a feminist. She seemed to abhor any expression of feeling but claimed to love Pollock and Van Gogh. There was always some other meaning snarling behind the stated one. Now, that hypocrisy had transferred somehow to Philip. That duplicity. And, thought Francine, it fit him well.

"He's holding a grudge and I don't know why," Francine would plead to her parents. Those were, her parents protested, the very same things he said about her. Verbatim.

As she opened the door of her house, she couldn't shake the sense—it prickled the back of her bare neck—that Philip knew something about her and Alexander, and that he was on his way to tell her.

9

FRANCINE, HIGH SCHOOL.

On a Friday, a day off from school, she took the train and then the bus and then another bus. Looking out the window of that last bus, she was quietly dismayed. Every vista brown and dying, the atmosphere appropriately grimy.

I am about to commit a crime against decency, she told herself again and again. She would not be accused in this life or in the next of having been unwilling to face the truth of what she was doing.

She had memorized the map she'd printed off the internet so thoroughly that she felt she'd been to this place a thousand times before. She imagined that she had entered not only another part of her province but another country altogether, the trip long enough to shed all her other selves. This might as well be England, she thought. Walking along the road's gravel shoulder next to ditches filled with lacy white and jagged violet wildflowers, she felt a kind of rightness.

She arrived at the end of a long driveway leading to a small stone house. It was far from the main road and she couldn't see any other houses nearby. This was the country. Where there couldn't be anonymity there was isolation, she observed, and smiled. Lately, she had begun congratulating herself for every one of her thoughts that seemed remotely true.

At the end of the long driveway sat Howie's little Volkswagen Golf. As she neared it, she saw that it was covered in loose maple-leaf keys that had fallen from the very large tree shading the front lawn. She stood at the door and knocked. An inner door opened, causing her heart to beat so hard she thought it might inflate her chest with panicked air and she might float away. She closed her mouth, then her eyes. She opened them.

She couldn't tell from his expression whether he was surprised or not to see her. He was rumpled in a faded polo shirt and khaki shorts too big for him. His stubble was growing out. His hair was longer than it had been, and there was a streak of white trailing from his centre part to the ear where he tried to tuck it.

"Hi," she said. She did not know how to address him.

"Turkey," he said, leaning out of his initial surprised—or was it hostile?—posture. "What are you doing here?"

"I came to see you," she said. She had determined earlier that it was best to be disarmingly frank. Her honesty would confuse him and thwart his attempts to steer her with insinuations or implications. "You said I could come to visit. You invited me here."

She perceived he was trying to suppress a smile.

"I really need a glass of water," she said.

"I guess you'd better come in," he said.

The house was very small, a single storey, almost as small as his apartment had been, the inside of which she'd seen only at one Bible study. She took off her flip-flops. Grime and her suntan left white lines across her toes. Past the foyer, the room was messy: books were piled on chairs, records in crates sat around the room, a spinning CD tower was wedged with jewelled cases, and there were potted plants hanging in the rough netting of macramé. She approached one of the piles. Books on theology, books on devotion, actual Bibles, books of poetry. She picked one up and looked at it, but wasn't able to take the words in. She had wanted to come into his home like a documentarian, for each moment to be held inside her, pure. She was making some memories. This was a phrase she'd said sarcastically to her girlfriends at parties or concerts—*let's make some memories, gals*—but there was nothing ironic in it now. She meant it. But now she found she was unable to properly *see*. Instead of sight she had feelings, shimmering at the edges of her vision. She could not look at him—so much for being disarmingly frank. She followed him to the small kitchen, where he filled a glass with water from the tap.

"This is well water," he said. "It's delicious."

"Well water," she said. She drank it all at once like a child. "Thank you."

He filled it again and passed the glass back to her. "How did you get here?"

"I took the train and then a bus and then another bus," she said.

"And then you walked all the way from the bus station."

"Yes." The water was helping.

"No wonder you're thirsty," he said.

"I came here to see you," she said.

"Yes," he said, laughing. "I gathered as much."

"Where is Sheila? Where's the baby?"

"Not here," he said. "But never mind."

"When is she coming back?"

He stared at her, silent, shaking his head with a scold.

"I missed you," she said.

He locked eyes with her.

"Did you miss me?"

"I miss all you kids," he said. He pulled his hands through his hair, a gesture she knew well, so well that it was as if he were performing it for her benefit. "I'm going to have to call your parents."

"You can if you want," she said. "But they're libertines."

"Your parents are libertines?" He laughed again. "What do you think *that* means?"

"It means they don't care what I do."

He frowned. "I'm sure that isn't true."

They both went into the living room with its infestations of books and plants. She was too aware of her arms, unsure how to hold them. He went over to the CD tower, held a square case, flicked the case open.

"When will Sheila be back?" she said.

He shook his head. She loved his hair loose like that. Mop-top, she thought; long and parted in the middle, shorter at the back. He looked younger than before, even with the grey. The shorts were terrible, but he was still tall, still had enormous hands. "She won't be back," he said.

"What do you mean?"

"The move has been hard on her. She and the baby are staying with her parents for a while."

Francine didn't pause to wonder, back then, if this was evidence of trouble in his marriage. She knew nothing then of the accountability marriage entailed. Marriage surveilled and trapped people much more than parents did teenagers, but her teenage self felt no sympathy for Howie. He was an adult, and as far as she was concerned, utterly free. She did not understand that he was much more thoroughly chaperoned than she was.

Surely he knew that by allowing her to come inside when his wife was gone—well, surely he meant something by it. And he had mentioned his address to her the last time they'd spoken, the possibility of a visit. He had let her in. It was what she and her friends called a *move*. He'd made a move; and now she was making a move. How to overcome the distance between them? What to do with these hands?

"She's not here in Perth?"

"Not in Perth," he said.

He put a CD into its circular tray and slid the player closed. She stood on the other side of the room with a book in her hand.

"Do your parents know where you are?" he said.

"Don't worry about my parents," she said. "Can I take a shower?" Her flip-flopped feet were dusty. Her face was sticky. "It was a long trip."

In the shower, she touched every part of her body as though it were bruised. She treated herself carefully. She felt she was being initiated into what people were capable of. She needed time and her body to tell her what was happening. Was this really happening? How could it be true that on the last day of your eighteenth year you were not capable of consenting, and then twenty-four hours later, as if by magic, you were? This is why people have initiation rituals, she thought, humming, the water pouring over her; and why, in an absence of widely accepted initiation rituals, we individuals invent our own.

Again, Francine surprised herself with this thought: her wit, her intelligence, her serious emotional depth. Sometimes when she came up with something wise, the pleasure was as delightful as a marijuana high or an orgasm. It doesn't matter how much you know—the insights rolled over her, cascading now—your knowledge changes nothing about your behaviour. I'm aware I'm a monster and still it does not stop me. But why is it monstrous to be in love? Who does it hurt? She loved herself, but it wasn't enough. She needed others to love her, she needed the impossible beloveds to be unable to resist her. The shower was a reset, a chance to try this again and to take a different tack.

Francine returned to the living room in shorts and an old Nirvana t-shirt she'd brought with her, her hair dripping wet and soaking through the shoulders of the t-shirt.

"So, Fanny, what are you doing here?" Howie said.

She hooked her thumbs into the belt notches of her cut-offs. Dre had liked this pose. Other boys had liked it. She wondered how much experience with women Howie had, and just wondering this made her ache and swell, made her lower body pulsate.

"I'm here because you wanted me to come."

"The last time I saw you I believe I told you to go home."

"I don't think you meant that," she said. She must have seemed to him filled with confidence, but inside she felt that she was shrinking, her bones losing mass. "I think I might swoon," she said.

"I've never known anyone like you," he said.

"Really?"

"I don't think you know this about yourself," he said, "but you're transparent. You are really not pretending."

"I'm capable of pretending."

"I'm not sure that you are."

"Really? That's how you see me?"

"As open, transparent? Sure."

"No one else sees me that way," she said.

He was standing near the stereo system. She asked him who the band playing on the CD was. She'd heard the name before; it meant oldie Canadiana, boring folk-rock. But in later years she would scour their albums to find the song now playing, its sweet predictable guitar lines, its subtle percussion, its proclamations of love. The song was called (hilariously, she thought later) "Ahead by a Century."

"Do you think you know me?" she said. She tried to take in her surroundings as she spoke. The wood of his furniture was teak, a honey shade she would not have a name for until she was married to Jamie. The walls had no paintings or even colour; in this, his house was unlike her own home. Her mother had placed art everywhere, although in every other way she was a minimalist. In Howie's home there were no relics of his wife, no baby things. A wind chime hung outside the screen door and she could hear the gentle clattering of its pipes knocking into each other. Howie just stood there, watching her, and it struck Francine that the books around him, his CDs, his records were filled with words and meanings, just as the two of them, looking at each other, were filled with thoughts and intentions. How tempting to burrow into this moment and never come to the end of its layers of meanings, never come even to the beginning of its story. She thought, not for the first time, about Jesus saying, gently, *Mary.*

You know my thoughts from afar, she thought. The light breeze and the wind chime made her feel that time was indeed slowing down. This was the delirium of falling in love, she thought. This was what we were made for, if we were made.

"I think I know you," Howie said again. "I'm flawed in many ways, but I'm pretty good at reading people."

"No one really knows anyone. I am not transparent."

"You are not transparent. That's not what I meant."

"I am opaque," she said. Her words were like oars driving her farther from him with every push. She resisted their momentum and walked towards him. She went to him and when he turned she moved closer, leaving only as little space as could be left between two bodies before they touched. He pulled her in, then, for a jocular hug, the front of his body turned sideways. What did he want? She presented her face to invite him to kiss her, and he nearly did, moved in close as she closed her eyes. Then suddenly, she drew away. "How can you do this?" she said.

He leaned back, took a step. "You're right."

"But I want to. *I* want to. It's just . . ." She could not speak the impossible question. How could he do this and still remain himself?

Howie looked down at her. The cotton sleeve of his t-shirt was touching hers. "I'm really confused, Francine, and a mess about a lot of things. I'm confused." He paused, then said, "This is more than I should be telling you."

"You can tell me things. I want you to tell me things."

He patted her arm. "I know I can."

"Adults like to pretend that people my age shouldn't be taken seriously."

"Is that so?"

"Please just kiss me," she whispered. "Please." She closed her eyes and could feel him coming closer. Then his lips were on her lips, pushing softly into hers, wet. He held her face in his large hands and kissed her. She sucked his lips into her lips, she pressed her tongue at his. Her arms were tight across his back, and she imagined she could climb his body. He smelled of aftershave, but his face was stubbled and scratched hers. She wanted not to think but only to have these sensations. Softness here, warmth, smells earthy and warm and *male*, scratchy, wet. Only to feel these things, and not to think.

He stopped. She felt him lift his head away from her and she opened her eyes to see him gazing at her. It was this gaze she wanted inside her. But the warmth of his assessment cooled, like the movement of clouds over sun.

"We'll stop this now," he said, hoarse. "I'm sorry. I shouldn't have allowed this to happen, Francine. I'm sorry."

He was moving away from her, one step, another step, out of her reach.

"I'm not a child," she said.

"Certainly not."

"I'm not even a virgin."

It was humiliating, to have to make so many gestures. She felt the infinite particles in the room suspended, waiting. The song was still playing, with its melancholy nostalgia for lost youth, and she felt it then, too: melancholy nostalgia for her own youth.

What did she even want from him—the man standing there shamefully by the stereo system?

"You can't take it back," she said, finally. "You wanted to kiss me and you kissed me and you don't get to take it back."

"I disagree."

"No, no, you're wrong," she said, and she saw him smiling. "I don't even believe in God," she said. "Nothing matters to me. You aren't *my* pastor. We're just two people." She knew it gave him pleasure, as it gave her, that she could be so surprising. Her hair was still wet, and once in a while a cold droplet fell from her head down her back. She wanted his big hand on her back, for it to slide down her back.

"Everything is permissible for you, yes. But not everything is beneficial," he said.

"Exactly."

"People don't just do what they want. The world doesn't work that way."

"Oh, I guess I don't know anything about people and the world," she said.

"Francine," he said.

She considered her options: continue arguing with him? Take off her shirt? Walk toward him? He was lying to himself. Religion was shame and deprivation. It was shame and deprivation, but it gave you *higher meaning*. So what? So did love.

"Why don't you teach me how the world works, then?" She pulled the shirt up over her head. Would he find her disappointing? Her breasts were medium-sized, her bra big and white and unsexy. Her skin mottled itself with something like a rash. Her face, her neck, were hot.

He went over to the curtains and closed them. "Francine."

She reached her arms behind her back and unhooked the bra, letting it fall down. He returned to her and pulled her naked torso to his wide one, his man's thick body, as though to cover her from view. She lifted her face to his again. Against her belly she could feel that his penis had hardened inside his pants, and it gave her a sudden wave of nausea. She pushed herself tighter against him.

"You're scared," he said.

"I'm okay," she said.

"Are you sure?"

She put her mouth on his mouth again. Focus on kissing and not on other things. Not his penis, not to worry about that yet. *This* was desire, to feel outside of your body and to fuck—even thinking that word made her so wet that she wanted to reach her hands into her shorts. Maybe to fuck would be the way to return yourself to your body. Maybe this was why you needed another person.

"Is this what people do?" he said, pulling away from her to pull off his own shirt. His chest was coiled with a pattern of curled hairs.

"I don't know," she said. "Is this what they do?"

At every step he ensured she was okay, ensured that he had permission to cup her breasts, to touch his mouth to her nipples—*stop talking*, she said, *everything is fine, I'm okay with everything*—but he didn't believe this, and he kept asking. She lay back on the couch and pulled off her shorts. It didn't feel like wanting anymore. The wind chime so close by, knocking, clattering gently, so gentle.

10

PHILIP, PRESENT.

The world was falling apart and the people who could do something about it didn't care. Six years ago, when he and Francine were still talking to each other, she had argued with him, that smug look on her face. Her features cinched in judgment of him. She told him, Read history! Read philosophy! Read a novel! The world has *always* been falling apart, she told him, it has always been evil and immoral. People do whatever they can get away with. That is what people all over the world do. Nobody with power is motivated to change the system; nobody without it can. She gesticulated, she furrowed her thick eyebrows, she implied, always, that he was an idiot. As always, she seemed to think she had described the whole system underlying the way the world worked, had tied it up neatly in a box, now to be put away on a shelf like memorabilia one had no need for.

The arguments between Philip and Francine had, for a long time, been civil. The two of them discussed ideas with a passion even their mother approved of. Their brother Steven did not have this passion, and neither did their phlegmatic father. Nor did Francine's husband or Philip's own wife, and so none of these others participated. It was Philip who had changed all that, five years ago. He had broken open the womb they all pretended to be cocooned in.

Now, standing on the back deck of his home, surveying his property like a king, Philip thought: the world *is* falling apart. In five years, how many species of the world's animals would be extinct? Already there were droughts and pestilence and famine and floods. There would be wars and rumours of wars. The world would get hotter, as humans filled the atmosphere with poisonous gas. And now there were two types of people: those who acknowledged this and did something about it, and those who—by their words or actions—showed that they did not give a fuck.

Philip's yard extended back fifty metres, but was only ten across, like many of the yards in this gentrifying neighbourhood. Plots had been divided and divided again, each a cell, and every several square miles you found one very large home—an estate, the home that had once overlooked all this land and called it one's own. Well, that was a lie, anyway. In the earth many griefs were buried, many wrongs. First Nations people had been driven out from here as they had been from all parts of North America, driven out and killed, or in various insidious ways "absorbed." It made a white settler who cared deeply, as Philip did, feel the guilt symbolized by his ability to live safely, to traverse the asphalt and concrete of this place, to walk the lawns, and to have succeeded all these others upon whose sorrows he trod. Francine accused him of white guilt and liberal guilt—but weren't these the appropriate feelings? He had been raised to have more than he deserved at the expense of others; he didn't blame his parents, with their work ethic and good luck, but reparations were certainly owed. He stood on the deck with his mug of coffee and breathed in deeply. He tried to imagine all that he could not see: the bay and its cliff edges not far from him, the highways clogged with cars going back and forth from the city, the sky above, the earth below. In the yard his two hens chuckled and scuffed the earth inside the pen he'd built them. His family had a daily source of fresh eggs from good, happy chickens; this was one gesture in the correct direction. Francine was the hypocrite, not he. Francine and Jamie, with their fair-trade organics in their coffee shop, pretended that they weren't capitalizing on the ethical awareness of consumers; he knew they were using these products not because it was ethical but because it made them money.

For the most part, over the last five years, Francine had ceased to cross Philip's mind; he had banished her as one does any negative fixation. But then, a couple of days ago, he had got a message from Sherri, their classmate from long ago:

—*Ran into your sister this summer—she was with the cutest guy out here in Huron County. I guess your mom still has that cottage? But she won't add me back on Facebook for some reason.*

—*Hey, Sherri,* he replied, *I guess that was her and her husband. Very handsome, yes, and a nice guy too. Don't worry about her not adding you. You know Francine.* Just like the old days: he had to clean up after his sister, to make excuses for her bad behaviour.

—I go by Sheryl now. Hopefully run into you soon! Always nice to see how well you're doing . . .

HE PUT HIS mug down. For the past five years he'd been a stay-at-home dad, learning all he could about sustainability. Kristal's law career supported them, and now, at thirty-four years old, he felt that if you looked on the surface of things, he was the success story while Francine and Jamie were still struggling. Of course, it was important never to take surface for reality. But here he and his wife were: in tune with each other sexually and spiritually, each of them pursuing good work, harvesting fresh, honest eggs, raising a pretty, happy, well-cared-for daughter.

But these messages from Sherri had unsettled him. They were like a poison that spreads slowly through the brain before it kills you. Had Francine and Jamie been at the cottage? As far as he and Kristal were aware, Francine hadn't gone to the cottage in years. Did his mom know? He wouldn't ask her, not yet, not until he'd spoken to his sister. Or at least sussed out the situation and come up with a plan for what to do. He put the mug down and packed his laptop and books into the saddlebags of his bicycle. Francine's end of town was only five miles from his end of town: they were pretty much the same large end. The only way out was through. He'd go and see her for himself.

—

IF HE ENVIED them anything it was the coffee shop. He loved what they had done with the place, the nineties vibe of it, the smell of espresso, the feeling of people gathering for conversation or to read and think. He tied up his bike at a rack outside Café Augusta, near a man and his aging husky whom he had seen out there before, taking advantage of the bowl of water Francine and Jamie put out for pets. The man with the husky wore a bright-orange visibility vest; Philip had once been the captive audience for the list of safety reasons behind this choice. He nodded, but the man ignored him this time.

In the store he saw the young baristas, and, by comparison, wizened Jamie, busy with a hissing milk steamer. He scanned the shop. At first he didn't recognize his sister. She was wearing a big sweater, sitting at a table reading the newspaper, her hair completely chopped off. Having spotted her, Philip went to the counter and ordered a cappuccino. He watched his brother-in-law tense up—Jamie must have recognized his voice—before turning to him.

"Hey, Philip! How are things?"

"Great, brother, how are you?"

The two kids who worked there looked at him with that open, scrutinizing expression all young people seemed to wear.

"Is that everything?" said the kid working the till. "We'll bring it out to you."

He nodded and turned away from the counter. An early alert system had been activated: his sister knew he was here. She was looking at him now, and he studied her face. She was aging, as was he. They were both wearing the marks of their expressive lives around their eyes and mouth. Her hair looked awful, he thought; she looked like she'd been through a round of chemo. And the cut made her look even more like him. Her eyes widened as he sat down at her table.

"Breaking your own rules again, huh?" she said, raising her eyebrows. "Very rebellious."

"Let's start out the conversation with antagonism," he replied. "The Francine Way."

"Well, it's just that you made such a thing of it," she said. "With your big rules of avoiding your terrible sister."

This had been a bad idea. The better part of him thought about leaving; last time he'd crossed this boundary it had taken him weeks to recover, as though his sister caused an allergic reaction with lingering effects.

"I'm glad to see you," she said. "It's just, you know, it's hard to be the terrible one."

"I never said terrible."

Five years ago, they had both used every word that came into their minds to wound each other, like frantic archers reaching for a cache of arrows. They had both said hateful things.

"We'll agree to disagree," she said.

"It's certain that we'll disagree," he said.

What to make of the fact that the person most like you in the world despises you so much? Francine had said once that by nature of their twinned genetic codes the two of them were inversions of each other, naturally repellent substances. Or magnets that pushed apart.

"I wish you enjoyed my hostile sense of humour," she said.

Jasper arrived with Philip's cappuccino and set it between them.

"What are you doing here, Philip?" Francine said.

"Honestly?" he said. "I'm worried about you."

She did not respond and looked away. A conversation between two young men at a nearby table swelled. They were students, discussing Sartre and their thesis advisors. "I take offence at her theism, to be quite honest," said one.

"I'm worried about you quitting your job, quitting school," Philip said, drawing his sister's attention back to their own conversation. "Quitting teaching."

His sister gave him a look that was both wounded and full of rage. It was an expression he'd often seen before, but only recently understood. Through his years of therapy he had come to the revelation that while seeming to have no boundaries, his sister had boundaries in the extreme. She did what she could with words and facial expressions to hold him off, to keep him at bay. *Don't even think about touching me.*

"I appreciate your concern," she said drily.

"Do you?" He picked up his cappuccino and sipped.

"How's the coffee?" she said.

"Great."

"Really?"

"I think so," he said.

"Yeah," she said. "People are full of implicit bias. And almost nothing else. We don't see anything except what we expect to see."

"Uh-huh."

"You expect it to taste good, but you don't actually taste it."

"Right." He shifted in his seat. "Well. Do you remember Sheryl Macguire? Sherri?"

"Uh-huh."

"She was trying to add you on Facebook."

"Was she?"

"She said she ran into you and Jamie," Philip said. "In cottage country. A few months ago."

Francine narrowed her eyes without speaking. But it didn't matter what she said now; he had seen the truth on her face. She stood up and the table shook, upsetting his cappuccino. He braced it with his fingertips.

"Why do you do this? You come into my life," she whispered, "at the worst times. The absolute worst times. You think I can just take it. You think—you have this idea that I'm strong."

"I don't think you're strong. I know you're not."

She looked like she might hit him. "No, you think I'm weak and you like to kick me when I'm down. I can't possibly handle you right now."

Then Jamie in his apron was beside them. They were, all three of them, taller than most people; and Philip was tallest. He took a final dramatic sip of the creamy mug and began gathering his things.

"I'm leaving," he said to Jamie. "No one can control her. No one ever could."

"Hey, man," Jamie said. "*Control* her?"

"Get the fuck out of here," Francine hissed. Her nose was red, like an upset child's, and her eyes brimmed with tears.

The students discussing Sartre had quieted. Philip slid out the front door, which slammed shut behind him. Of course—to make the place seem rustic, Jamie had installed a screen door without springs. They just let it bang back on its frame like that. Philip unlocked his bike and wheeled it down the sidewalk.

His sister always made him feel that he had done something wrong, when *she* was the one. She always got him to say the thing he didn't mean—he didn't mean that she should be controlled. He didn't think that, didn't believe that, didn't think women should be controlled. No, he didn't think that at all.

11

FRANCINE, HIGH SCHOOL.

"What is it, turkey?" Howie clasped her forearms, her elbows.

"I'm scared," she said.

"Me too," he said. "I think . . . It seems like . . ."

"It seems like what?"

"Like I should know better."

She said nothing.

"We can stop if you want," he said.

She pulled his wide torso towards her. She lifted her face and kissed him again.

"It's okay to be scared," she said. "I think it's okay." Everything she said startled her—he was making of her something new, just as the Bible was meant to do, as the Lord was. With him, she was suddenly in a new and different loop. His admiration made her beautiful, intelligent, wise. She wanted to tell others about what she felt, about this new way of being. Kids she saw at parties, Philip and his friends, the kids at the youth group. But who could she tell about this particular surprise, that age doesn't matter? It doesn't! *It's not age or gender that necessarily gives a person power in a relationship*, she thought (and much later, she would try to defend this revelation). *It's something else, something more particular.*

Now, they kissed each other tenderly, he with a sweet nervousness, she with trembling expectation. Sometime later he suggested that they have lunch, and he led her to the kitchen where she watched him work at the counter, arranging breads and cheeses onto a plate, placing olives on a platter with his large fingers. These easy gestures made everything feel real. She wanted to say something like, *This is the first time I have felt present in any moment, I think this is what is meant by love.* She said nothing. He walked over to where she sat at the table near the window and put the platter down.

He smiled, putting an olive in his mouth. The empty backyard framed him. A tree in full summer green, a maple with arms that seemed to sweep around slowly in the breeze, like tentacles in an underwater scene. In the autumn, it would flame out and disrobe. It would ice over and then it would pimple with little purple buds, and then once again grow the long green tentacles of summer. The tree was a vision. It was unclear how much time had passed. Still the platter was full of food, still there was an olive at his lips.

Observing these deliberate gestures, his quiet speech, Francine recalled the official version of him. Offering bread, pouring wine, saying *take* and *eat* and *remember* and *believe*.

"I don't believe in God," she said.

"I know."

"Does that bother you?"

"It doesn't bother me," he said.

"Why not?"

He picked up a slice of thick bread and buttered it. "I'm not sure about my own beliefs anymore."

She took the bread. She brought it to her mouth and inhaled its yeasty scent. She bit into it and chewed.

"Sheila will be at her mother's for a while," he said. "She claims that she will not come back. She took Justin with her."

"She took your son."

"She hates that I moved her to this place," he said. "And now I have a congregation to answer to, a somewhat old-fashioned congregation that will have trouble with divorce or separation. Or maybe I'm not giving them enough credit. I guess I don't know what they'll think. Sheila kept using the word *gulag*. You brought me to a *gulag*."

"'Gulag,'" Francine said. She nearly laughed. One woman's gulag, she thought. She would have done anything to be incorporated into his life, here in this place. The books and music, the olives, the cheese, the macramé, the maple tree. "I have this fantasy," she said. "Of having no ties."

"Like no family?"

"No ties of any kind. I want to just move from place to place and know nobody. I'll move to a place and plant a garden and then I'll leave."

"Why a garden?"

"I don't know."

"A garden is quite a commitment." He seemed amused. "And what about love?"

"What about love," she said, bending her head, trying to seem thoughtful. "Does love have to tie us to anything?"

"Yes."

"I just think it would take a lifetime to understand just one thing. Just one single thing. And if you spend that lifetime distracted by people . . ."

"But people are your life. You are a person."

I will believe in this, she thought. This new way of being.

"I want you to tell me your whole life," she said. "I want you to tell me everything that ever happened to you."

"You sometimes remind me of an alien life form," he said. "In a good way."

She felt a sudden wave of revulsion. He was somebody's dad, embarrassing them both with these stabs at humour, this clumsy flirtation.

"Don't make fun of me," she said.

"You don't really want to hear about my life, anyway," Howie replied. "About my boyhood and my parents, my faith and how it has faltered, how I thought about becoming a fireman, a policeman, an astronaut, and how I ended up here in this kitchen in Perth, Ontario, staring at you."

He looked at her and she looked away, back at the tree. "I'm sorry," he said then. "I shouldn't have said that. I guess there's a lot of things I shouldn't be doing that I am doing. Things I'm saying."

She put her hands on the rim of the table. She felt as if everything now was happening because she had willed it. An awesome, awful power. They would have to break free of each other, or else just give in to that power. She stood up and came around the table, closer to him. "If you were a fireman," she said, "none of this would be an issue."

"Because it wouldn't be wrong?" he said. "Or because if I were a fireman, you wouldn't be interested in me?"

"You think I'm interested in you because you're a pastor?"

The next words he said stuck with her long after.

"I think you're ambitious. I think you need someone who doesn't give in too easily."

She was standing over him, and he tipped his head up to look at her. She said: "When you say things like that you sound just like every other person."

He put his hands on her hips; she put hers on his face and bent over to kiss him. He was briny from the olives. He breathed in heavily through his nose. She sat on him, one leg on either side of his waist. The mound of his penis grew and hardened. She thought of pornography she'd watched on video: of a female teacher who wears a bra that leaves her nipples uncovered, glasses sliding down her nose, her excitement at a hard cock. In the video, the woman spits on the man's cock. How easy it was to find the control panel on a man and manipulate the dials.

She wanted Howie to slide into her.

When he was about to come, he turned into someone other than himself. She closed her eyes as he grunted and panted and then, gently, before she herself could finish, moaned. Where was the wholesome person who had seemed to know and hold the truth? Was this person, overcome with hard desire, the real person—and everything else an act? Was the animal more real than the person?

If you let one thing out, everything else tumbled out too. If you took off your clothes and showed a person everything. If you gave a person your body. People did this sacred thing every day. But each person was a closet packed too full with stuff. Everyone was gated but could be unlocked.

Later, Howie made them coffee, chattering on, zipping his shorts back on, sending her to the bathroom to pee. She obliged him, worried that to do otherwise would shame him, and shame might lead to anger, might lead to him kicking her out and then where would she go? She splashed cold water on her mottled face smeared with mascara, smeared raw by kissing, by someone's sandpaper face. Don't be so dramatic, she thought. Splashing cold water on a face was a TV show gesture, a Hollywood trope. What had he done that was so wrong? He had, kindly, told her to pee.

But his face looked stricken when she returned to him. "I don't know if this was right. Is it right to follow your heart?"

She felt those words in the pit of her, coiling.

He had faith, he had doubts. She listened to everything he had to say. She sat on the couch, throbbing and still unsatisfied, legs tucked under her. She felt like she now possessed some great, worldly wisdom. She sipped the coffee he made for her and listened as he went on and on. The curtains in his living room were still closed. It was evening, the first day.

"Shouldn't you make sure your parents know where you are?" he said at last, ending the flow of words.

"I told you they don't care," she said, more harshly than she meant. Better to be sad than ashamed.

THAT NIGHT, HE held her. He pushed her hair back from her forehead and said, "You know, we're all debris."

"We're garbage?" she muttered, feigning sleepiness though every part of her was awake. She was wearing white underwear and a white t-shirt. There was a tiny spot of stickiness below her belly button, and she kept touching her fingers to it, as one probes a toothless socket with the tip of the tongue. His woollen blanket made her too hot and she pushed it off.

"Not garbage. But we're all exploding from that first star, that first big bang, whatever it was. We're all bits of matter coming apart from that explosion. It's happening at an incredible speed," he said.

"'Incredible speed,'" she said. Her hand was on his chest, her leg draped on his, as though they had been lovers for many years. After a moment, he stood up, smiling down at her as one does at an overly keen student, apologetic and annoyed. She watched him in the faint light from the wide window at the back of his bedroom. He slid the window open.

"Are you going to break my heart?" she whispered. "I don't know what's happening."

"No, no. Never," he said. He traced his large hand down the centre of her chest, like a surgeon readying to make a cut. He pushed the blade of his hand down and pulled her shirt up.

"A person as broken as me doesn't know how to do that," he said.

But she felt afraid. Maybe it was the cold air lifting her skin out of itself, pores popping up, as he put his mouth on her stomach. She was too old to be Lolita. Even when she'd been ten, eleven, twelve she'd felt old, too old. Her face had never looked innocent, she'd never had the innocence of Philip, his loose mouth ready to be smacked. But now she longed to be older, to be many years older and Howie's peer, to have lived long enough to understand this moment, for this to be her future and not her present, not a thing done and hurtling away from her.

He had already been inside her. Now he slipped his fingers into her panties and touched her clitoris. As he did, he raised his eyes and looked at her uncertainly.

"I wouldn't do this if I wasn't sure you were ready." His eyes shone at her in the near-dark. Later he'd tell her he felt possessed. He'd beg for her forgiveness and ruin everything.

"I'm ready," she said. "I'm fine."

ON THE GREYHOUND, heading home, she pulled her legs up to her chest and stared out at the endless landscape. As a child she had been excited to see cattle grazing in the fields. Her mother would drive her and her brothers through the countryside to the cottage, pointing out the animals. Had she really once been thrilled by such things? Now, seeing these cows in the distance, flicking their long tails, she felt as if she was travelling away from herself. She still felt full of him, of Howie. She glowered. Now her life would be reduced to a series of orgasms. Already she could define herself against the orgasms she'd had alone; these ones with Howie were the first she'd had with another person. These latter were moments of embodiment; everything else was nothing but the wispy falsehoods of her mind. So this was life, she thought, this was love. One other person and no one else for miles, just you and him in a house. Making love. This was the secret, and now she was privy to it.

Before today she had felt that she wanted to be devoured by Howie. In that Tim Hortons months ago, she'd begged him to take her. He'd resisted. But now he was enfeebled—as she was—by desire. It seemed to her now as if he had moved away to that small town specifically to make this moment possible. And this was proof that the truth of the world was sex, not God. Despite her lack of belief, she experienced this as a loss. Was the truth of the world only bodies and desires and their satisfaction? Or maybe desire was the route to God. There was a mystery here that she wanted to tug on like the fraying edge of a piece of cloth, to make it unravel and reveal. She felt the mystery but could not access it. Her mind spun, and she could not hold on to one thought before it was on to another. Heady with feelings, she sat back and listened to a mixtape of songs on her sporty yellow Walkman. He had promised he would call her, he would write, and she looked forward now to those promised bits of contact. She relished the memory of his hot breath in her ear: *love, love, love*. On the turf of her seat on the bus, her head leaning against the window, the music allowed her to quietly cry.

HER MOTHER WAS waiting for her.

Victoria dyed her hair a formidable dark brown, and styled it, most of the time, in a chignon. She wore pencil skirts and shoulder-padded blazers. Though Francine and Philip knew that she spent most of her time grading papers and preparing lectures, this work took place in her office at the university and was invisible to them. Tonight, she was at the kitchen table in her casual weekend wear: a cardigan, to replace the blazer, over a polka-dotted blouse, the rest of her outfit hidden from Francine by the cut of wooden tabletop. A glass of red wine was in front of her. She looked at Francine with arched, thin eyebrows. "And where have *you* been?"

Francine had not considered that she might need to explain herself, and she realized she didn't want to lie. What was the worst that could happen if her mother knew the truth? It was Saturday evening. Pastor Howie would be in his house, trying to write a sermon. She had asked him earlier that day if he felt like a hypocrite, and he'd shaken his head. It would not surprise Jesus that he was no paragon of virtue, he said. But now, in this new context—her mother's kitchen—Francine felt the strangeness of these words. She thought of the round, smooth dome of his penis's tip, beading stickiness where it cracked open. She tried to shudder the thought of it away. It had become ugly under the kitchen pot lights. She should have kept her eyes shut and allowed herself to only feel, not see.

"I was visiting my boyfriend," she said, tingling with the thrill of scandalizing her mother.

"Oh, you have a boyfriend, do you?"

"Yes."

"Does he go to your school?"

"No."

"Do I know his parents?"

"No," she said, and sat down across from her mother, mimicking her pose. She put her forearms down, elbows out, on the flat surface of the table. In response, her mother withdrew her arms and crossed them over her chest.

"What makes you think you can spend the night at your boyfriend's house without clearing it with me?"

"I cleared it with Dad."

"Your dad said that you told him you were sleeping at Mya's house."

"Right. So what's the problem?"

"You lied."

"I'm eighteen," she said. "May I have some wine?"

"Oh, why not!" Her mother suddenly stood up and walked briskly to the counter, where she grabbed the bottle of Pinot Noir and yanked out its loosened cork. She poured wine into a glass and placed it in front of Francine with so much force that the wine almost splashed out of the glass. She sat back down and stared at her daughter. "Go ahead, drink."

Francine picked up the glass and sniffed it. The sharp, sour odour: it made her want to puke.

"So, what? You think you're in love?" Her mother caught her eye, and Francine felt that she could see right into her, surveilling her like a machine. *I know you, Francine. What did you do this time?*

A thought came to her: Oh, God, what if it is true that men can desire you even if they hate you? What if Howie, even good Pastor Howie, could fuck her without loving her?

She was aware that she was losing control of her gestures, radiating uncontrolled emotion with her secret. "What are you upset about, exactly?" she said. "Does it bother you that I'm interested in men? Or does it bother you that I'm eighteen and I can do what I want now?"

"Oh, nobody gets to do what they *want*," her mother said. "That's the first thing you'll learn."

"Tell me all about it. Tell me about my whole life," Francine said. Philip came into the room then and sat down between them.

"You are not eighteen for another two weeks," their mother said.

"Can you give us some privacy?" Francine said, turning to her brother.

"He can stay," her mother said.

Francine tipped back the glass and downed the wine. It burned her throat, then came back up, momentarily, into her nose.

"You said *men*?" Philip said.

Francine nodded.

"Men?"

"What are you getting at?"

"*Adult* men? A man?"

Francine sighed.

"What is your boyfriend's name?" Philip said. He wore what Francine interpreted as a smug look on his face, the look she hated most. She feared more than almost anything that she also made this face. That his face was her face.

"His name is Humphrey Bogart," she said.

Her mother shook her head.

"His name is Tom Cruise," Francine said.

"What is it really?"

"There is only one man in the world," Francine said. "One man with many faces."

"You can't be serious for even one second," Philip said.

Francine stood up violently and grabbed the wine bottle and refilled her glass.

"That's enough," her mother said, clutching Francine's arm to stop her, as if suddenly frightened. "That's quite enough."

PART TWO

I discovered what people are capable of, in other
words, anything: sublime or deadly desires, lack of
dignity, attitudes and beliefs I had found absurd
in others until I myself turned to them.

—ANNIE ERNAUX, *Simple Passion*

12

FRANCINE, FIVE YEARS EARLIER.

"Sometimes the roof blows right off the house," Francine said to Simon as he clutched at her. Simon tugged on the strap of her damp black one-piece, nearly revealing her breast. She tried to hold him against her hip. Sand was working into the creases near her bikini line, under her breasts, between her toes. She'd have raised red bumps later. The lake had already been tossing and stormy, more grey than blue. Clouds churned, and the wind was so powerful she could hardly open her eyes.

"It's like Kansas or something," her father said. "I've never seen a storm like this in Ontario."

But the wonder for Francine was that after everything the family had said to each other by then, they were all, somehow, still alive. And she blamed her mother for everything.

∞

ON THE FIRST day at the cottage, her mother had fed them potato salad, chicken salad. Only later did she mention that she'd been horribly sick with a stomach bug. "I almost didn't make it," Victoria said, as though sharing incidental news.

Francine thought of her mother's hands preparing the meal. She and the other young mothers she knew were always trying to manage their children's periods of exposure and quarantine, to achieve the correct balance of these. "Why didn't you tell us you were sick! We can't afford to get deathly ill right now."

"I'm fine now," Victoria said, regal and severe and a little defensive. "You're being dramatic, Francine."

"Yes, I *am* being dramatic," Francine said.

Philip stood up. "Don't talk to your mother like that," he said.

"Really?" Francine said. "Are you going to be your mother's great defender?"

"You can't speak to people like that and just get away with it."

Her brother was standing now, gripping the edge of the table. She saw how serious he was, but she felt her own rightness. And she felt furious. Despite how hard Victoria had always been on Francine, Philip would not come to his sister's defence.

"Are you sure about that, Philip?" she said. "I think maybe I can."

LATER, WHEN FRANCINE tried to remember the arguments of that weekend, they snapped towards her without preamble, without warm-up: a series of whips. The second afternoon, Philip had found her out back of the cottage with Simon.

The empty chairs were rattling in the rising wind now. "You think you can do and say anything you want and everyone's supposed to accept it," her brother said.

As Francine and Philip argued, Victoria sat nearby, close enough to overhear, beside the ashes of the firepit. Francine imagined that she and Philip both saw their mother as she wanted to be seen: upper-class, a sophisticate who went to art openings and had poets and intellectuals over for catered dinners. But they also saw the truths she wished to hide: that she had married a cabinet-maker with no ambition, that she had stayed married to him despite her constant irritation in his presence, that in spite of her often-stated liberal sexual politics she herself appeared disembodied—was possibly, Francine thought, asexual. She had once, in an unguarded moment, told Francine that she had a very low sex drive. The knowledge that she had nursed her children, had created babies in her uterus and pushed them through her vaginal canal: all of this was difficult for Francine and her brothers to square. Sometimes Francine speculated that something bad had happened to her mother; better to have an explanation than face the bald fact that your own mother is not capable of warmth. Damaged people damage people: a cliché her friend Maggie had once offered.

"I don't think I can say or do anything I want," Francine said.

"Not only that," Philip said, ignoring her, "but Jamie thinks everything you do is just fine."

"Of course he does," she said. "He's my husband and he loves me."

They were out on the lawn. Philip came closer to her, glaring. Simon crouched in the grass, looking up at them both with interest, without fear.

"Whatever you do, Jamie approves of it, he thinks it's just great. He never tells you you're wrong," Philip said. "That's not love. That's codependency."

"I'm not an alcoholic, Philip."

"All kinds of people, not just alcoholics, need codependents," he said.

"How can you say that—Jamie's the best thing in my life," she cried then. "Why would you say that?" Though she and her brother had shared a womb, they had not shared an egg, and her mother told many stories about how they had always fought: Philip kicked Francine from inside the amniotic sac; Francine screamed for attention whenever Philip tried to nurse. When Francine had been younger, she had accepted these tales. But later, when she tried to recall the dramas of her childhood, she did not recall any of this; she remembered only years of affection and love for her brother interrupted briefly by an adolescence steeped in disdain and pity. Even his hostility towards her now didn't track with what she had always believed about the two of them—that their affectionate parrying was never intended to hurt. She believed he was over what had happened with Howie.

"You're projecting," she said to Philip. "Because your marriage is so bourgeois. Because you are so bored by playing by the rules. Maybe *that's* not love."

"How can you say something so cruel?"

"But you were cruel first! You said that same thing to me, just now!"

"You believe it's not only okay but good to selfishly pursue your desires," he said. "And you think someone else's faith in something—in anything—is something to be pitied."

"Philip, I'm not the person I was when I was seventeen," Francine said. She lowered her voice, conscious of Victoria, there at the edge of her vision. "And you're saying things now that you can't take back." Her mother was listening smugly, as though speaking through Philip, as though he was her ventriloquist's doll.

Her brother was breathing heavily through his nose; it brought to Francine's mind a hot-tempered animal, a bull. Philip was taller than she was, but the differences between them were mostly due to hormones: his shadow of stubble, his harder jaw. They shared the same crooked smile, and she saw mirrored in his face her own lopsided sneer.

"There are things *you* do," he said, "that you cannot take back."

The sky seemed to descend on them then, with its thick soup of clouds. She thought she could see the air spiralling, could see the clouds begin to funnel. Wind tugged at her hair and sundress, which floated up and sucked back.

"You just love this, don't you?" Francine yelled, whirling to face her mother. Across the lawn, Simon looked up at her, eyebrows arched. There was no one at the firepit.

Ashes were in her eyes, stinging her throat. "Is this still about Howie?" she said to Philip. "Still about youth group?"

"Don't act innocent."

"I'm not. I just—I truly don't understand."

"My faith meant everything to me, and you didn't even think about how your actions might affect me."

Francine stifled a whimper. She wanted to plead, pitifully, that she'd only been a kid. Instead she aimed her words to hurt him: "Why is this about *your* faith and *your* purity? As though *I* could corrupt you."

∞

FOR THE REST of the weekend at the cottage, Philip refused to speak to her. He became a ghost possessing the house. Francine would catch fragments of his presence, venting to her mother, her father, his wife: "*not* forgivable, *not* forgivable." His voice filtering thinly through walls, always sounding like a child's whine to her even though it had the depth and range of a grown man's.

When her mother came into the kitchen and said primly, "Well, this was a foolish idea," Francine contained her response, said nothing. She gripped Simon firmly against her waist, though hours of anger had weakened her. Her son's skin, like her own, was filmed with sand, and that sand rubbed against her skin. He played with her hair, which was still damp. "Mommy, Mommy, why does the roof sometimes blow off the house?" he asked.

Eventually the radio warnings had calmed. Francine's parents went to sleep in the main-floor bedroom on the other side of the house, the children were piled up and sleeping on the great-room floor, and Philip was off being grouchy someplace out of sight. Francine sat with Kristal at the dining table, one drinking wine, the other sparkling water, a jigsaw puzzle spread out in front of them. Francine's belly was large enough that she had to sit a little farther than usual from the table. Jamie was there, too, or—she couldn't remember exactly where Jamie had been. In the upstairs bedroom, near the toilet, throwing up by then? Huddled, shivering, in a blanket near the table where she and Kristal sat in the dining room?

Kristal was a lovely, small-boned person, as unlike Francine as Jamie was unlike Philip, a person who seemed naturally to spill over with kindness, untroubled by questions of purity or corruption because they didn't apply to her. Kristal never raised her voice at her daughter, never clenched her jaw or fists, never even seemed to frown. Francine hated that this good woman was witness to all that was bad between her and Philip, and she attempted now to make jokes like short cloudbursts to ease the pressure. The two of them talked tornadoes, potential and actual; they talked about the logic of staying downstairs and in a central room. They admitted to becoming more aware of the construction of the house, the advantages of crawl spaces versus basements, outer windows versus inner door frames. Francine's mother, before going to bed, had gone around the cottage taking paintings off the walls and stacking them in the crawl space.

They took sips from their glasses and moved their fingers around, searching for pieces, the three remaining adults—or had it been just the two of them?—at that dining table, pretending that Philip's anger was of no great concern, behaving the way normal people might do at normal cottages.

"Kristal, I love him, I love him the most," Francine said, unable to help herself. She could not stop revolving through the paces of the argument.

Kristal looked up at her. "He's your brother," she said. "I know." Kristal feared nothing, not even her.

"I'm going to go outside for a minute," Francine said. "Get some air."

The company that owned the corn in the fields and sold it to farmers for feed had nothing to do with her family—and yet here the corn was, an army of giant stalks swaying toward each other companionably. She had not yet met Alexander. She was still young. Her hair was long, peaches and cream, the colour of good corn. Philip, she could see now, was in the upper rooms of the house. He had turned on all the lights and left the curtains open. When they'd been six or seven, Francine had sent Philip into the cornfield. She bet him he would get lost if he went in. And he had gotten lost. After a few minutes, she'd screamed his name, running along the edge of the field and back again like a dog agitated and trapped by a fence. She screamed until her mother found the path he'd taken by following the broken arms of the corn. Now she realized that Philip had not forgiven her for that bet, either. It was one piece of his proof that she was the evil twin. The crops returned every year, the whole unbroken army. She felt her brother staring down into the dark, unseeing and sure in his opinion of her.

Earlier that night, Francine had lain with Simon while he fell asleep. He'd demanded that they lie down further away from Celine, his cousin, and he dug his feet into the space between Francine's knees. He had asked her again, "Mommy, why does the roof sometimes come off the house?"

That was when she'd seen the stupidity of what she'd said earlier, saw how it would give him nightmares. For months Simon had been afraid of many things. Would wake up inconsolable. She could not stop his night terrors even if she pinned him down, if she took him by his small shoulders and shook, if she pleaded, "Mommy can't take it, you little monster. Mommy can't take it." *Sometimes the roof blows off the house.* Why had she told him that? "No, no," she soothed. "The house is much too strong for that. The house is stronger than the wind. I'll keep you safe. I'll never let anything happen to you."

Just because you knew a lie when you heard it, that didn't mean you knew anything about the truth. The breeze stirred the corn. The corn whispered and swayed. She imagined she looked like a farmer's wife: barefoot, hair braided but wild, enormously pregnant. The unnamed, ungendered baby she had only seen in the grainy pixels of an ultrasound moved within her, and she went back around to the other side of the house, to where the children were sleeping in the huge living room, hoping to wake Simon so that she could hold him, to reassure him, to reassure herself, that they loved each other and that love like this was enough.

But there was her twin in the dark against the wall, Celine's head on his lap, Simon's near his feet; all of them sleeping. It was too hard a world for Philip; it was too hard a world for Simon; it was too hard a world for any child. She went to where he was sitting—her twin, her double, her dearest self—and she struggled her huge body down and sidled up close. She rested her head on his shoulder and his eyes opened. She saw them flash.

"Don't you dare touch me," he hissed.

13

PHILIP, MEANWHILE.

A perfect July day. The air was warm and stirring slightly, rippling the edges of his mother's tablecloth, picking up strands of Kristal's hair, of Celine's, of his nephew's. The children were angelic in the late-day light. The willow tree drooped behind him. He and his family were newly vegetarian, and his mother had accommodated this, but even so, Philip was edgy with nerves. Across from him, his sister's eyes roved from the food on the table to their mother, then rested for a moment, wasp-like, on Celine's face before flashing back to his mother. Francine didn't look over at Philip. Perhaps she could sense that something was going to happen. Or maybe she'd be good, for once, and he wouldn't have to come for her. All things are possible, all things permissible—but those old Bible passages were no longer anchored to any meaning and, floating through Philip's mind, confused him. Francine's hair was absurdly long, like a hippie's. She wore a flower tucked behind one ear. He'd watched Simon give it to her, plucked from the wildflowers growing in the banks by the willow, and watched her beatifically receive it. Under a tight black jersey dress, her belly was enormous, her face rounder than usual.

Philip remembered his mother scolding Francine years ago, when she was pregnant with Simon. "For a woman of such good looks and intelligence," Victoria had said, "you really don't know how to put your gifts to use." This had provoked Francine's usual fury. "I'm not scolding, merely observing," their mother had claimed.

As lunch went on, Philip heard Francine start to gripe about Victoria's snobbery, watched as hostility tensed and swelled between his sister and mother. He let them toss their mean words around for a time before interjecting.

"Francine doesn't believe in anything, so I wouldn't bother talking to her about this," he said. "Also," he said, turning to Francine, "treat your mother with some respect after she just served us this beautiful meal."

"I suppose you're about to propose a toast?" Francine said. "Or should we have said grace?"

"What?" Heat rose in his face. He clenched his teeth.

"Are you a Christian again, come to judge us all?"

"Better that than an utter nihilist, like you," Philip said.

In a cartoon, they would have both risen from their seats to confront each other, nose to nose, sending the spread clattering from the table. They would have proposed a duel.

She was ugly in her rage, as he knew he must be ugly in his.

∞

THE NEXT DAY the storm came. But even before the sky turned green, then purple, trouble swirled. At lunch the day before, Victoria had told them she was getting over the stomach flu; that next morning, Simon grew sick. After breakfast, as Philip sat with his parents drinking coffee in the great room, on one of the couches dwarfed by that room's size, Francine burst in, cradling her toddler in her arms. "See what you've done." She was blotchy with tears. Simon leaned over her arm and vomited right onto the hardwood floor. Francine screamed, "This is too much!" She was wild-eyed, a cornered animal, her son attached to her like a lower mammal. A sour smell filled the room.

"I'm sorry for Simon, but *we* didn't do this," Victoria said.

"Francine," their father said, gently.

"You're all standing there yelling at me while I'm crying, while my baby is sick!" Francine wept.

"It's not our fault," Victoria said.

"And you're the one yelling!" Philip yelled at Francine.

She sniffled, cowering, as though they had really done something to her, and Philip saw in her pose what looked like shame. She was embarrassed by her outburst, he thought, and for a second he pitied her. She was like an animal, abandoned to her instincts.

"I hate you," she said. "I hate all of you."

After that, Victoria got on the phone and told Steven not to come join the rest of the family, as he had planned. Francine was quite unstable. Steven, the first-born who had received the birthright, floated above the rest of them like a gentle god, never to be touched by the enmity between the twins. Kristal begged

Philip not to get involved. "We shouldn't act like this in front of the kids," she said.

But Philip followed his sister outside, where she had taken Simon to nurse.

"It's all my fault that my child is sick, right?" she said. They sat near the firepit in flimsy, foldable lawn chairs. The wind was colder than it should have been. "Now I'm the one who ruins everything. Ruined Mom's birthday. Now it's all my fault."

"Sometimes—" he tried. "Sometimes you do upsetting things, Francine, or the way you react is—"

"What?" Her shoulders shook and she began to sob. "You came out here to accuse me?"

"You *are* at fault sometimes," he tried.

"I need you to be kind to me right now."

"Everyone is always kind to you, and you lash out at them."

"Please just leave me alone, please."

"I'm not leaving this time."

She lifted her whimpering child to her breast, unlatching the top of her dress and bra, not caring that he saw. She held Simon's forehead with a palm and shushed her child. Philip reminded himself that she was a mother—she was a small child's mother—a giver of life, of nourishment. Jamie loved her, her child loved her.

"Sometimes people do things that are not forgivable," he said.

She kept her gaze fixed on Simon and would not look up at him. The wind was so strong he could hear the corn stalks cracking.

"Don't you think?" he said.

"Are you asking me to agree that I am unforgivable? No, I guess if I assented to that I wouldn't be able to live so, no, I *don't* think." She looked at him then, her face clenched with the effort of trying not to cry. Like a child herself. Appearances were deceptive, he thought: this was no mother.

A chair lifted lightly a centimetre off the ground, as though pulled by a very big magnet, and then fell over. Philip stared at it, rage at Francine, her self-pity, stoking inside him. "But that's not what I said, I didn't say—"

"Kids!" Their father was at the back door, gesturing wildly. "Come in! It's about to storm!"

HOURS LATER, AFTER the tornado warnings ended but the rain continued to pour down, Philip could not remain calm. He put his fist through a wall, then he took the car out for a drive. He pushed at the gas pedal, gouging the mud-soaked driveway with his tires, and sped down what the family called a highway, although it was only a country road. His knuckles hurt where the skin had torn off, and it hurt to clutch the wheel.

A hundred, two hundred metres ahead of him, Philip saw a small car fishtail. He watched the weak red lights of the car's backside leave its lane. There was a semi driving toward it, toward them. Philip waited for a collision as the wipers flew across his windshield and back, the rain so heavy that the motion only seemed to shovel water from one side of the glass to the other. Unable to see ahead, Philip sensed that he had disappeared into the path of the truck. He waited for it: a mechanical sound, a blare of horns. But nothing happened, and a second later he saw the semi pass him. That was enough to make him turn around, feeling lucky and shaken, wanting to hold and be held by the ones he loved.

But when he came quickly back in through the front door, into the foyer with its banquette, its bouquet of sunflowers, bouquet of daisies, several old dining chairs, visitors' book, he heard his mother say, "This is no place for children."

"What place is a place for children?" Francine's voice said.

"You need to care for children. You have to protect them."

Then a door slammed. Philip tried to find his way back to what he'd just been feeling, his longing and gratitude and love, but instead there was the hole in the wall, drywall collapsed on itself, and he felt afraid. He looked down at his fist, which was painful to clench. No one had even noticed he'd gone. He found he didn't want to cross the threshold, as if he were a person in a horror film or a bad dream. As a child he had sometimes pictured Francine as being possessed by evil, frenzy in her eyes, blood wetting her long hair. He had been afraid of what might happen were this apparition to appear, had frequently been unable to sleep as he waited for whatever lurked in corners or beneath furniture to come cutting at him. His mother, too, he could imagine as ghostly and malevolent. There had never been anyone to go to for help.

Now he began to pace in the foyer. The argument with Francine had unearthed something—and wasn't that what horror stories were all about? You were supposed to let bad things die and remain buried, not dig them up. Maybe he had been wrong to seek therapy and try to work this all out; maybe it was better to deny and repress and manage. It wasn't as if he expected his family dysfunction to resolve. But he had needed help. In truth, he always had. As a teenager, he had *needed* Jesus Christ. Had needed the Holy Spirit, that dove. Even the maniacal Creator God with all His caprice. And he had needed Howie, needed to be taught to pray. *A prayer of petition means you are asking for help,* Howie had told him. *If you ask for a fish, He will not give you a stone.*

He couldn't go past the threshold.

Philip heard murmuring voices, then the sound of a body rising from a chair, moving toward him quietly, footsteps padded by socked feet. He stood and waited at the inner door. Kristal: her kind, calm face.

"Baby, what's wrong?" she said.

He didn't know how to answer her, but seeing her gave him the strength to move into the house, and past the table where Jamie and Francine were doing a jigsaw puzzle while the sky outside, above the house, whipped everything to shreds.

Francine said, sarcastic, "You need help with your bloody hand, Fip?"

And then Philip was flying up the stairs. There was no one up there, no kids in beds—the storm had scared them all to the main level. The rain pounded the roof. He found some ointment and a clean bandage in the bathroom, and washed his hand with a baby-blue shell-shaped soap. His hand throbbed, and sweat on his brow began to drip into his eyes. He returned downstairs to the great room, where a wall of windows looked out onto the cornfield. The kids were on the floor in a pile of blankets. His footsteps had roused his nephew, and he sat down between Simon and Celine with his back against the wall, patting and shushing him back to sleep.

The rain had stopped while he'd been dressing his wound, and through the window he could see Francine outside in the yard, walking up and down along the edge of the cornfield. The sky was bright with moonlight, but his sister looked lost. She looked unlike herself. She pulled at her length of hair and tossed it over her shoulders, looking up at the sky. He thought in that moment that he loved his sister and could forgive her. A great love there was for a twin, a self that was not a self; and hardly anyone else knew what this was like. Not a parent and child, not a wife and husband. Just the two of them, him and his twin.

He thought again of that brief time, so long ago now, when they had gone to youth group together. He was reminded that for her thesis Francine had tried to write about Mary Magdalene. Maybe, after all, there had been some love for God in her. *They have taken away my Lord, and I do not know where they have put him. They have taken my Lord away. Oh, where have they put my beloved?* Maybe they had both been pacing and begging for there to be a God back then, each in their own way. What if he'd never gone to the youth group? What if he'd become like his mother— the way his sister had—using his mind like a knife? Where did this softness inside him come from?

Francine had turned and was looking at him through the glass. She walked around to the side steps and he heard her open the door. Then she appeared, barefoot and muddy to her shins, still wearing that jersey dress—or wearing that jersey dress again—her hair wild. She saw him there on the floor. He wanted to forgive her now. But he knew that if he gave in she would always be the one who got away with everything, who always got what she wanted.

She came over to sit with him, resting her head against the wall. "I miss being a little kid sometimes," she whispered. "A little kid entranced by a sky, by a cornfield, by a storm."

Why did she think she could just sit down here and pretend, as always, that nothing had happened? When she moved to touch his arm, his wounded and bandaged hand, he recoiled.

PART THREE

A gust of godlikeness may pass through you
and for an instant a great many things
look knowable, possible and present.
Then the edge asserts itself.

—ANNE CARSON, *Eros the Bittersweet*

14

FRANCINE, PRESENT.

Alexander's hand on her back, her waist, his lips on her cheek. Lust was an irritant; she had a week to get through before she could see him again.

She bought a pack of cigarettes one day, and drove her car too fast another, as though either of these things could help take the edge off how she felt. She smoked, like a teenager, behind the brick wall of a churchyard near the boys' school. And she smoked like an adult in the alley behind the café, where Jasper would come out sometimes to heave a black garbage bag into the dumpster and bum a cigarette. She didn't mind if Jasper saw her smoke, or if Jamie did, but she wouldn't let any children or women in the neighbourhood see. The women were a village, policing her. She smoked on the back porch when Red and Simon were at school, sliding the butt through a crack between wood planks. She told herself she would only smoke one pack, and then it would be Friday and she would see Alexander. What she needed was a hobby. Or she needed her profession back. She washed the nicotine smell from her hands and tidied the kitchen, the living room. Dropped trucks and dolls into baskets, returned throws and cushions to their spots on sofas and chairs. Then she was in the yard again, closing her eyes. (Alexander in the library stacks, asking her about poetry. "A woman taunts her lover," one Lawrence poem began. "You've a warm mouth," another says. She'd memorized these words so she could move her mind over them and over them. Like a troubadour. Feelings, feelings, feelings. *This*, she had thought, or I'll throw myself out the window!)

And now what? She, still alive, surveyed the backyard: the hedges overgrown around the back perimeter, the patchy grass where her sons liked to jump in big soggy puddles, where plastic figurines of soldiers and fairies were buried. The flame of her match flared. The sky greyed toward winter. Her trouble was that she couldn't figure out who she was. That had always been the trouble. If Howie could have told her; if some handsome boy could. Or was she Jamie's wife, a mother, a woman, a friend? She was a woman. Old enough that there was no excuse.

She pulled her phone out of the pocket of her wool coat and thought about sending Philip a message. Her confusion was *his* fault. Even though he thought it was *her* fault. That she was to blame for everything. She opened her messages and found, buried, an old thread of their communiqués. *Hey Pip*, she wrote, using an ancient nickname. Ip. Lip. Fip. *Remember when we were babies*, she wrote, then deleted. *Hey Pip. Was nice to see you yesterday.*

If only there were a window to jump out of.

She opened her contacts on the phone and found "H." Just H. It probably wasn't his number anymore. She closed the phone.

Across the alleyway, she could see the backs of houses, romantic in the grey light. Attics and chimneys. Tall brick houses bulging with badly matched additions, so that the brickwork formed zippers. One of those attics was infested with raccoons. A fat, matronly bandit climbed out of a tree and picked up one of her babies and then another with her humanlike hand, its finger-like claws, and tossed the baby like a shotput ball onto the neighbour's roof, where the baby raccoon clambered into the chimney. The matron didn't notice Francine sitting there, her face pluming smoke. Perhaps she was a machine in some other mammal's thoughts. Perhaps she was a distant house on fire.

Because of the business and the school community and the small size of the university village, she and Jamie were well-known in this part of the city. There was a small-town expectation of good citizenship. Probably she ought to tell the neighbours what was happening in their attic, but she wasn't about to have that raccoon murdered.

She opened her phone again, scrolled to H and pushed the icon to send a message. *Is this still your number?* She watched the chat screen for long enough to see a bubble appear with its throbbing ellipses, the promise that he was typing a response. She waited; the ellipsis continued to throb. *I have so much I want to tell you*, she added. She sent this and the bubble was gone.

How would this end? So much for sublimating desire. Maybe she should get some bonbons and read Proust in a soft armchair. For now, she went inside to masturbate in her marital bed, which she hadn't even made. She pulled the blinds so that the room was dim as a teenage boy's basement bedroom, as a place where you went to buy drugs and be hit on, and this feeling of wrongness wove into her fantasy, too: Alexander at the grocery store, Alexander at the cottage, in the library on a desk, Alexander licking at her pussy—she came quickly, and was more bereft than ever.

"WHY IS PHILIP suddenly showing up at the coffee shop? When's the last time you talked to him?" Unlike Francine, Jamie never showed his exhaustion by seeming harried. He sat at the table she'd made after taking care of every task she'd needed to do that day, despite her reveries: dinner of chili and buttered bread, the boys at the table, homework finished, happy enough to see their father.

"I don't know. At least a year."

"What's gotten into him? He doesn't look like he's well."

Francine agreed—despite feeling a kind of hatred for Philip—but she was stung a little by this remark. It's not that he's unwell, she thought, it's that he knows something you don't know. She wondered if it would make Jamie unwell to know she was having an affair with a first-year university student—but she couldn't imagine him taking the news with anything other than his calm stoicism. *Yes, that's Francine for you, always getting into mischief.*

"I didn't like seeing him," Jamie said abruptly. And then he asked the boys after their day.

"Red said a bad word today," Simon said.

"I did not."

"He said *stupid*," Simon said.

"I never did."

"Let's not use that kind of word," Jamie said.

"Daddy, I didn't!"

"Who don't you want to see? Who came to the store?" said Simon, whose seriousness was undercut by the ring of red sauce around his mouth.

"Don't worry about it, kiddo. Just the tax man coming to take more than he's earned."

Francine laughed. "Exactly."

Francine had met Jamie seven years after the last time she'd seen Pastor Howie. A string of affairs with several other older men had ended with the owner of a bar where she was waitressing, post–teacher's college but pre–supply teaching job. Martin was forty, balding, and exuded a yeasty stink of beer. By then she had come to believe that her particular form of brokenness was detectable to anyone who'd want to exploit it—the way pedophiles were said to know which children would be easy to lure and to shame. She saw herself as a semi-broken child who appealed to assholes. Men her age seemed not to notice her at all.

Jamie had saved her. Jamie matched her in smarts and age and looks. Jamie wanted children; and he wanted to have them with her. With Jamie, she felt she could reject volatility; he had calmed the storm that had opened up inside her. And for a while, she did seem to be cured of her restlessness. It made sense to them both to get married, though she had often said she didn't believe in marriage—and soon after they were married, frequently suggested amicably divorcing. Marriage only seemed to happen, she mused, because you were so high on love chemicals and hormones that you'd agree to anything.

"Marriage suits me fine," Jamie said in those days, before children. But he was also cheerful about her doubts. He had been raised by such good and generous people. The salt of the earth. They had formed him into a man of sanity and security. "I like your company," he told her.

"You like my eccentricity."

"That too."

"You know how they say no one should make any big decision during the year when they are grieving?"

"Yes."

"I think that's also true of the year after falling in love."

"But then it would also be true of many things. One could never make any big decision."

That was how Jamie had talked her into getting pregnant with Simon. It was during those innocent days when she'd loved nothing better than to lie half-awake with her hand on his cock all night. When she hardly remembered that Howie had ever existed.

"Traumatized people don't recognize themselves in a mirror," she said to him once, when they were talking about children.

"How could that be true?" he said.

"We can't have children," she said on another one of those days. "Not until I'm finished my Ph.D."

But by then it was too late.

ON THURSDAY, SHE woke her sons up early when she spotted the raccoons coming out of their compost bin.

"Aren't they supposed to sleep during the day?" Simon asked.

"They're so cute, Mom. Mom!" Red in his pajamas with sleep in his eyes. He seemed in his delight to be accusing her of something. "They're kind of weird, too, Mom. Right?"

Posed there, with her children, Francine felt as if she was presenting the mother raccoon with a mirror. See? I'm not the lazy do-nothing you think I am. The idea that she should pull the kids out of school and teach them at home gripped her, as it sometimes did.

"Are they nocturnal?" Francine asked. "I guess maybe they are." She had gleaned this only from children's books she'd read to her sons, books she'd read herself as a child—and it suddenly seemed to her that children were the only stewards of these kinds of facts. A black sky, bright moon, stars. Things known about dinosaurs and the solar system.

"We aren't going to kill them, are we?" Simon, at eight, was filled with moral purpose. He had not forgiven his parents for putting out a trap for a mouse, and when that didn't work, borrowing Maggie's cat to kill it. Francine had found the cat on their bed with an expression on its face she could only describe as lusty—like a vampire's. The mouse's head was gone and the cat, otherwise an underwhelming greyish-brownish house cat, was licking the very red, open body of the mouse.

"We won't kill them," Francine said. Why show a child anything about the world when everything passed by, died, hurt you, killed you in the end? "Let's get you boys ready for school."

And what would she do if her sons, at eighteen, had sex with a teacher twice their age? She liked to put her teeth into that thought. It was Jamie's favourite thing about her: she would allow herself no delusion.

She decided that it would be fine. As fine as anything. So: not fine. Fine, not fine that Simon was growing out of his babyishness, his little lisp, his chubby hands becoming long-fingered like

Jamie's, his eyelashes, his dear eyelashes, less lustrous. Fine, not fine that it was coming for Red, too. No one stayed a baby for long. They'd make their choices and their mistakes and, like her, they'd be fine. How else could you be a mother? They'd be fine or they wouldn't, like her, like Jamie.

15

PHILIP, HIGH SCHOOL.

Two weeks before Philip turned eighteen, he'd followed Francine to the town of Perth. It wasn't difficult. She hadn't exactly erased her trail.

A few days earlier, he'd watched, just out of earshot, as she'd talked to someone on the family phone. As she spoke, she looked happy in a way that turned his stomach—smiling and dead-eyed, like a person too high on drugs. Her expression reminded him of a photo he'd seen in a book on Jungian psychology, showing a group of people in a state of weird religious ecstasy. The telephone had a small screen that would light up with numbers, and after Francine hung up, Philip pushed redial to see the number of the person she'd been speaking to. Later at dinner, to test her, he brought up Pastor Howie's name, wondering how he was, and whether they should go together to visit him.

She confessed nothing. That was her confession.

"You must miss him, too," their father said, turning to Francine.

"I hardly think about him," she said.

Philip carefully gathered the evidence. And on the day she went to Perth, he was following slowly in his car behind her city bus, as though he were being towed by the bigger vehicle. Other cars veered around him as the bus stopped and sighed and sighed and stopped. He watched Francine get off the city bus and onto the coach at the depot. That was when he knew for sure where she was headed, as he had looked up Howie's address. In later years he was amazed that Francine hadn't known that he was following her. His yellow K-car was in rough shape, and had windows tinted light purple by a previous owner. There were psychedelic decals on the back windshield. That Grateful Dead teddy bear. But he remained unseen. In Perth, he waited down the street from Howie's little house and watched Francine come around the corner and stride right up the front walk. He thought about the phrase "love is blind," and wondered if it meant not just that you couldn't see your beloved's flaws, but that you couldn't see anything but your beloved at all.

After she went inside Howie's home, he tried to calm himself. He couldn't decide if he felt sorry for his sister for being possessed by evil or hated her for being unable to resist it. *He* could have resisted. And why, of all the good people to corrupt, had she chosen a person that *he* loved, a pure person, innocent? He felt victimized—just like Bathsheba's dead, forgotten husband Uriah in the Bible. In the end, David had hardly been punished for killing a man out of mere lust. Instead he was immortalized as the one after God's own heart, the bester of giants. Philip felt a growing outrage now for the injustice of his own situation. It was as though Francine was doing this to spite him, to spite Philip, to pollute his love for Howie.

They didn't even close the curtains. He saw his sister and Howie move against each other, and that was enough. As he'd been driving, he'd thought that things might end this way, but he hoped that instead he'd see Howie pushing Francine away. He imagined Howie saying sorry and closing the door. Philip would retrieve Francine and drive her home.

But Howie had let her in.

How many times had he sat in Howie's office, nearly crying but unable to weep? Howie had been patient as Philip lined up his worries. His eyes kind as an old dog's. He had proffered explanations from the scripture, and comforts: the Lord will not tempt you beyond what you can bear. They had prayed together, heads down and solemn. About women, Howie had reassured Philip that he would find someone. But if Howie were willing to do this to his sister—didn't stop himself from sinning—then he didn't believe in limits, and there was no hope.

Philip started the car and it backfired loudly, but he didn't care. He raced away back home.

Howie's actions—his sister's—were audacious, and perhaps there was no God after all. It broke his heart. An abuse of power, Satan delighting in pleasure, teeth. For ten years, Philip felt this heartbreak. Before, he'd taken comfort in a vision of the close beneficence of a watchful God. Now this God was wrenched away from him, the illusion shattered like a glass under a mean heel.

"One bad man does not nullify the power of God," his therapist said, when Philip was in his thirties.

"And what if all men are bad?"

"That does not necessarily nullify the power of God," the therapist repeated. But she did not believe in God and could not convince him of the value of his faith. She pretended tolerance for it, that was all.

On the day he followed Francine to Perth, Philip saw that God's power *was* nullified if righteousness turned out to be impossible. This loss nullified goodness, which nullified God's power or proved God's power to be corrupt. Or maybe proved that there was no God at all.

16

FRANCINE, PRESENT.

It was Thursday. Francine's friend Maggie was back in town, briefly, from a year of living in the desert in California. *We have so much to talk about*, Maggie texted. *I'm living a Leonard Cohen song. I* am *Leonard Cohen.*

Ah, women, Francine thought. She took a gulp of cool air, felt a rush of relief as Maggie arrived at the café. Maggie's large presence, her buttery voice.

"Look how tan you are," Francine said.

"Yeah, well, I was in the desert," Maggie said. She gestured at her wavy hair. "My hair was straight for months."

"Really?"

"And *your* hair?" Maggie put her hand on Francine's shorn head, the back of her neck. A chill sparkled up Francine's arms.

At the counter, Jamie welcomed Maggie to take any pastry she wanted, but she shook her head. "I'm in love," she said, "so I've lost my appetite. I will take a coffee, though."

In love, no appetite? Francine felt suddenly exposed. She suggested a walk to the campus instead of sitting in the café. The trees were heavy with moisture, leaves shining as if coated with fresh paint. "I've missed this the most," Maggie said. "If you can believe it. A cold, hard wind. The threat of tumult."

"I love it too," Francine agreed.

Maggie had met a man in Los Angeles while at a conference, she told Francine as they walked. She had been dazzled by the glamour of American academics, as she always was. Everyone in LA with their Ivy League educations. At the conference bar, she'd been talking to someone who defended Heidegger against Maggie's claims about his fascism. That's when a couple came in. The man, who knew the Heideggerian, had a slight Italian accent and was handsome in a poet-like way, a scarf around his shirt collar. The woman he was with turned out to be a famous actress, a regular on a major TV show. A show with a doctor.

Francine listened with mild interest, aware of her peripheral vision, of every student in a wool jacket with dark hair and a nice haircut. "That's rich people for you," she said. "Just like the kids at the school when I was teaching."

"Oh, right. All those entitled boys," Maggie said. "Flirting shamelessly with you."

Francine's neck went hot, and she put her hand on it. She'd forgotten that she'd told Maggie about that. She'd almost forgotten that it had happened. "So tell me more about the Italian and the actress."

"Okay, don't laugh. He comes from royalty. Really. He comes from Italian royalty."

Francine did laugh.

"And he's very handsome. So, we are at the bar and the Heidegger guy is there—turns out he's dead married and actually committed to marriage, but he is fascinated by polyamory and he starts talking about the Italian, whose name is Marco. And Marco is really looking at me because he *is* polyamorous. And soon he's asking me about my work, he's fascinated by my work, and the next thing you know I'm moving in with Marco and the actress in the desert. Cactuses everywhere."

"Is it cacti or cactuses?"

"I don't know. Hey, what are you so preoccupied about?"

"What do you mean?"

"The way you are constantly looking around. Are you expecting someone?"

They'd reached the campus, and now sat on a bench. "So, you moved in with the prince and the actress on a crumbling southwestern estate?"

"Uh-huh," Maggie said. "Changing the subject?"

"Sure. Because you left out the important part. I knew when there weren't any people in your Instagram photos that you must have met someone and were keeping it quiet. But how did you get from talking to the couple at the bar to living with them?"

Maggie smiled. "I don't know. How do these things happen?"

"You tell me," Francine said. "It's so baffling. How you get from being two discrete people and then suddenly you're kissing, then fucking, then making a life?"

"The fucking was incredible, I will admit. But it started to feel so unreal. Like it wasn't a real life at all."

Students were passing by their bench in pairs and clumps, or singly wearing headphones, eyes on screens, rarely shifting gaze to look at them.

Maggie paused. Then she said, "Francine, what's wrong? What's going on?"

"What do you mean?" She'd forgotten her mittens at the café and now she held one hand with the other to warm her fingers, clasping them as if she were a Barbie doll, stiff and formal.

"You look so stricken. Or like you're ill. And you cut off the Lady Godiva hair."

"I look ill?"

"You look sort of less buoyant."

Her awful lust was a kind of sickness, like nausea, heavy in her guts. Now she wanted to jump into Maggie's lap, straddle her, kiss her. "Did I ever tell you about Howie?" she said.

"Who was that?"

"He was the youth pastor at a church where my brother and I went when we were teenagers."

"Oh no," Maggie said. "Did he preach the purity gospel?"

"It wasn't like that. He wasn't a hypocrite."

"But he screwed around with you? Or your brother."

"We had an affair. He and I. I was the only one."

"As far as you know."

"Stop it," Francine said. She stood up from the bench. "Stop it."

"Stop what?"

"You're misunderstanding what I'm trying to tell you."

"I'm sorry. Go on. You had an affair."

"I don't want to talk about it."

"Please tell me," Maggie said. "Is this why you're upset?"

"I'm not upset."

"We don't have to put up with this stuff anymore, you know," Maggie said. "Men behaving terribly. Being shits. Groping us. Raping."

"I'm not talking about that," Francine said. Cold air travelled through the tweed of her jacket. None of her clothing would be enough to cloak her. "I'm talking about *me* behaving badly. *Me* behaving badly, and I don't want to stop, and I can't stop."

"Did something happen with the priest?"

"Pastor."

"What happened?"

"No, that was a long time ago, it's not that. I'm seeing someone. I—I fucked someone. And I feel some kind of attachment to him, and I feel how awful it will be. That it will end."

"You're in love."

"I don't think so. I'm having all the symptoms. But I am not in love." She felt desperate now to change the subject. "You're in love, though, you said?"

"Oh, no." Maggie laughed at her affectionately, teasing. "My sweet, sexy baby," Maggie said. "Poor you. Poor Jamie. Is it Eli, finally?"

"No, no. Not Eli."

"So we are both tragically in love, are we?" Maggie said.

Francine shook her head lightly.

"I hate the desert and I also hate polyamory actually, but Marco is committed to it, and so I'll go back, because of love.

Love means you run toward it no matter what, right? I want to feel that I would shatter my whole life for love. What else is there to live for but these infrequent hallucinations of transcendence?"

"So, you're going back?"

"I think so. I think I have to."

Francine felt a jolt of energy travel through her. Alexander was nearby. Her hands were hot. She looked at them: red. "Is this frostbite?" she asked Maggie, holding them up.

And then Alexander was there. He was walking toward their bench, and the leaves fell prettily around him. "Hi Francine," he said. His jaw with its slight cleft in the middle like the rounding of a peach, an ass, a vulva. She wanted to put her tongue on that smooth, slightly rough cleft. Was it love, this desire? If love wasn't desire, what was it?

"Are we still on for tomorrow?" he said.

"Friday morning," she said. To look at his eyes was to allow the jolt to run through her and down. "Oh, Maggie," she said, "this is Alexander. A former student. I'm tutoring him in Classics. See you then, Alexander."

"See you then," he said, gravely, perhaps mocking her. "Ms. Nichols." He walked past them and away, and she didn't watch.

"A former high school student," Francine said. "Very smart but terrible in Latin."

"A former high school student. One of the entitled boys?" Maggie said, squinting at her. "Are you good in Latin?"

"Better than he is."

"So you're his tutor."

"I can't—"

"This is very obvious to everyone," Maggie said. "It is leaking from both of you. It's blubbering out of you."

"He's not my student."

"But he *was* your student?"

"Men do this all the time," Francine said.

"Oh my god," Maggie said. "Don't tell anyone else about this. Don't tell anyone else and don't see him tomorrow. This is bad. How do you not know it's wrong?"

And Maggie edged away from Francine, slightly.

17

FRANCINE, PRESENT.

Francine texted Howie two more times, for the pleasure of watching that meaningful ellipsis, that slippery ellipsis, the typing and erasing, the considered pause. He didn't text back. Finally she wrote, *I need to see you. I need your help.*

On Friday morning, after she dropped the boys at school, she went home to shower and shave, trying to feel as if her body were perfect, invulnerable. Maggie called. Francine watched the phone buzz, unanswered, on the countertop as she dried her hair. She packed a little overnight bag, even though she'd be back later that afternoon for school pickup. She took what she'd need to put her body back together after letting Alexander take it apart.

She found his apartment. It was too near Philip's house, only two blocks south and three blocks east, the attic of a giant two-and-a-half-storey Victorian brick home. A person riding a bicycle flew past and glared at her as she stood outside. Alexander buzzed her in and she climbed three narrow flights of curiously winding stairs, as though the house had been drawn by Edward Gorey, designed by Lewis Carroll. His place was small and cozy, with a balcony and a small fireplace, and piles of books.

"This is more bohemian than I expected," she said.

"You think that because I'm rich I have terrible taste," he said.

"I missed you."

"I missed you, too."

"You feel okay about this, still?" she said.

"Of course I do. That night at the cottage was the best night of my life."

"Does it bother you that I'm much, much older than you?"

"It doesn't matter," he said. "Why would it matter?" He peeled away her coat as though spinning a top, to make her spin. He no longer seemed a boy. His sleek body under a fine soft sweater, those cuffed jeans. There was hardly a boy there. She moved nearer and touched her tongue to the cleft in his chin.

"I definitely feel okay about this, still," he said, and without asking began to remove her clothing. "I want to tie you to the bed. I want to blindfold you."

"Okay," she said. She would be his experiment. She remembered that sometimes she *had* felt Howie was too old, much nearer death than she was, nearly a corpse. Even when she'd loved Howie, she'd glimpsed this sometimes. Now Alexander manoeuvred her toward the bed. Still clothed, smiling benevolently down at her, he gently pulled a knot around her hands and attached them to his bed frame. He put his mouth on her nipples and sighed. His mouth on her breasts, wet tongue sliding over her nipples.

"Kiss me," she said.

"Say please."

In her purse, piled on the floor near the door, her phone lit up. A message from Maggie: *Don't do it. Come see me instead.* But she wouldn't get this message until later, walking into the cold, flushed with the thrill of Alexander. Perhaps her internal organs had collapsed, she thought then, because she couldn't breathe, she felt no hunger, and her throat was so parched that her voice came out as a croak when she thanked the bus driver and stepped into the street near the school to pick up her children.

Alexander pulled a large cool cloth over her eyes, and then his mouth was on her again, her nipples, her elbows, the fleshy bowl above her pelvis, pushed out like the clamshell Venus; he was pulling her knees apart, putting his tongue inside her. Sex could beat them both clean of their ages again, beat the outside world away from its persistent existence, push them to a brink together where there was only their bodies, their feelings, her wrists rubbing against the silk tie he'd used to bind her, the sensation, blindfolded, that he was touching her everywhere, that he was two men, that he was three or four ungendered people, and that she was helpless, surrendering. And the certainty passed over her, as the lust turned to fucking turned to coming, the certainty passed through her that this was love and that this (yes, please, yes, God) was the only thing.

18

—

FRANCINE, HIGH SCHOOL.

Howie mumbled in his sleep. His sleep-talking was unintelligible to Francine, lying awake beside him, and perhaps this was worse than if he'd been muttering *what have I done, oh, what have I done?* As if loving her was a crime so terrible. If he regretted loving her, she would be too lonely in this sad little house, this place to which his wife had abandoned him. She pulled herself out of the bed.

The wind chime rattled, even in the middle of the night. The flash of green on the stove read 2:08. Why did there have to be a world outside, beyond this house? Francine wanted there never to be anything other than this house. She opened cupboards, reading spice jars as though they were little bottles of medicine. As though it were a disaster film and she was trying to find the only antidote to the zombies, the only antibiotic that would heal her lover. Old cinnamon shaker filmed with dust. Half-empty basil with an avocado-green lid. Salt and pepper shakers probably stolen from a diner. A can of Campbell's soup . . . this reminded her of Warhol, which reminded her that there was indeed a world, a world in which she'd once taken a trip with a girlfriend to Toronto to visit the art gallery. A world in which existed Warhol's Elvis, Marilyn Monroe. She continued on her project, picking up a jar, looking at it, putting it down. Howie had woken up now and she heard the creak of his footstep, another footstep, and soon he would sit at the table and fix his eyes on her and ask, *What have I done?*

She wanted him not to touch her now, not to beg her for anything.

He was walking so slowly, creaking on those floorboards.

"Turkey," he said. He sat at the table. His face furred. His eyes too big, too hungry. He was about to say it.

"Don't say it."

"Turkey," he said again, and took a breath.

19

FRANCINE, FIVE YEARS EARLIER.

T windom made them a snake that swallows its own tail. When they were children, Francine had used Philip like a mirror: to see what *she* was feeling she'd watch *his* face for emotion. They had become those infinite mirroring puzzles: in his eyes she could see herself reflecting; in that reflection were his eyes. Together they were a strange loop, trapped in an Escher drawing where you think the stairs will take you up, but you end up down. They would never escape each other. He felt *her* shame; she loved *his* faith. And after the storm at the cottage, she knew he mistakenly thought the person he hated was her.

Jamie and Francine could never clearly remember the sequence of events that had occurred that week at the cottage; they compared versions of what had caused what, like children counting the days on their fingers. The tornado had funnelled close to the cottage, but in the end it had touched down only elsewhere, in a nearby county. All that came to them were intense winds and driving rain and a weird blue-green light illuminating the grass, making it look silvered, like metal. A hammock torn to shreds, an awning ruined, a swinging porch seat with its chains wrapped around itself. Rubbish flew into the yard and field: flyers and newspapers, dirty flattened plastic cups from the side of the highway that stuck in the corn and landed in the stream.

One of the days had been spent cleaning this up. A day had been spent vomiting (by Simon), and another day of vomiting followed (by Jamie). Francine counted it out: that was three separate days. There was the day with the birthday cake. The day Philip in his anger punched his hand straight through the drywall in the foyer, leaving a fist-sized puncture and white dust on the floor. A clock fell on its glass face and shattered. On one of the days, the cottage became no place for children.

Afterwards, her mother and father took Philip's side against her. "You know you're difficult, you have a mean streak," Victoria said to her a month later, from across the table at a café—what her parents called "neutral" territory.

"Philip was the one screaming at me!" Francine protested, unable to contain her tears. Her body was swollen with the baby and with preparatory milk. Blood flow increased in pregnancy; all her veins also felt tight and full. "Why don't you think *he's* difficult?"

"He says the same to us about you," her father said.

"He says, 'Why don't you think *she's* difficult?'" Francine said.

"Yes," her father said.

She stared at them. "But you do think I'm difficult."

They stared back at her. If only Jamie were here, he'd laugh. But she had come here alone and was outnumbered, as always.

"You have a temper," Victoria said. "You may as well admit it. It can be very difficult to be around you."

Her parents' faces were masks, the faces people wore when they were trying to be brave. They appeared to Francine to be genuinely afraid of what she might do.

"But *he* punched a hole in the wall," she pleaded.

The café was in her mother's neighbourhood, and its white-and-silver decor, its crisp lines, even its lack of coffee puns or kitschy coffee-related artwork, seemed designed to contain and cool tempers. There was no warmth. Not like Café Augusta, the coffee shop she and Jamie were in the process of opening. Now Francine found herself assessing her surroundings with the eye of a businessperson, an entrepreneur. This place was trying to do all the things that she would not. She would attract a clientele nothing like her mother.

She stood up abruptly. She and her famous temper—well, then, she would frighten them, she decided. She would threaten to knock over the table—and in that moment, she saw the masked courage desert her parents' faces, and horror in the movement of their jaws. She wanted to douse their laps with boiling hot coffee.

Letting her desire stand in for action, she stormed out instead.

After this, she and Jamie were left alone for weeks to try to figure out why her brother was so angry. Yes, he had given his reasons—but none could be believed. None warranted this level of ire. At nights during this time, she and Jamie lay in their large, comfortable bed as a fan oscillated, whirring, pouring cool air on their hot bodies. She felt like a wrestler after losing a grapple.

Though no one had touched or hit her, she felt the effects on her body. Around her eyes the skin was raw, irritated by tears, and then by her rubbing at those tears with whatever was at hand— her shirt, her mother's rustic tea towels—and her muscles had that shakiness that comes after a hard workout or a long run. She felt constantly dehydrated. And she and Jamie could not put the pieces of that week at the cottage together.

I have a toddler, she thought, and a baby on the way, and I can only remember what happened in flashes. What had happened and why: if only she could understand it, maybe she would understand everything. This was the foolish belief she held. Some secret must have been revealed—but no matter how hard she tried, she could not decode it.

One day, she newly recalled an incident that had happened at the cottage, and she turned it over in her mind for clues. She and Simon had been leaving the beach, walking up the long wooden set of steps her father had built when she was a child, when they came upon Philip blocking their way. She was aware of the buzzing of insects. A bee landed on Philip's hand, and he marvelled at it, then pointed excitedly at a nest that had been built underneath the step.

"That's a wasps' nest," Francine said, eyeing its papery construction. Simon, who was afraid of bees, was now crying, and Francine tried to bustle him up the steps, but Philip wouldn't move.

"Get out of the way!" she yelled. "Move out of the way!"

"This is not a wasp," he said, showing the insect on his hand. "What is wrong with you?"

"You always say *what's wrong with you? what's wrong with you?* It's an awful thing to say."

"Awful," he said. "I'm the awful one, right?"

"I'm so tired," she said. "Simon's upset. Can we just pass by?"

Wasps buzzed around them now. She felt the buzzing in her teeth. Her arm holding Simon was so tired it had turned numb. Very slowly her brother stepped back to let her pass.

"I know, Philip. I know how awful I am. I know I don't deserve any better than this," she said, trying to stitch a confession into an apology. "I don't like how I am. I hate how I am. I'm trying to be better." Because maybe that was the thing: She was mean and hard, and he wasn't. He liked to attract insects to his outstretched hand, and she wanted to bulldoze past him. She had a temper, and he was its victim. "You have to forgive me," she said. "I'm pregnant, and I'm exhausted, and I'm trying."

"You can't just—" he said. "It's always something with you." He shook his head. She put Simon down and held his small, warm hand as they made their way up the wooden stairs. She felt frightened to leave Philip behind her, watching her. She didn't believe he was capable of murder; but she also believed that, under the right circumstances, everyone was capable of murder.

She *was* mean. She *did* have a temper. She turned around and said, "We should tell Dad about the wasps."

He had his hands on his hips. For the first time, she could not read his expression. And she understood that something was about to turn.

20

PHILIP, PRESENT.

At dinner one night in November, Philip was typing messages through Facebook while Celine ate spaghetti and Kristal picked at a salad. "Do you think Francine will be okay?" Kristal said. "Your sister is always on the fastest collision course she can find."

"Hang on," he said, typing at the screen with his thumbs. He was messaging with Sheryl about the day she'd run into Francine at the store near the cottage. He described Jamie—"tall with glasses"—and asked Sheryl if this described the man with his sister.

Uncommonly handsome is all I remember.

Got it, Philip wrote.

Is Francine okay?

Oh, she always lands on her feet.

"Yep, fastest collision course," he said, looking up at his wife. She kept her fine hair in a bob, and was still wearing makeup from her day at her office. Pristine of face and body.

"We have a rule about phones at the table," Kristal said, holding her fork in her thin hand.

"Sheryl said that the man was uncommonly handsome. Is Jamie uncommonly handsome?"

"Sure, I'd say so. Sure."

He stared at Kristal. "Oh, you would?"

"You asked."

He looked a little Greek or Italian or something, Sheryl wrote now. *I hope Francine's okay.*

His daughter's spaghetti, which had only a few minutes ago been neatly coiled in a small, colourful bowl, now hung from that bowl's sides. "Daddy?" she said, an outline of sauce around her mouth.

"Celine?"

"Why are you talking about Auntie Francine?"

"Because I love your Auntie Francine."

"Then how come we can't see her?"

"Don't talk with your mouth full, sweetheart," Kristal said. "She misses her cousins. You miss your cousins, don't you?"

"We've talked about this, Kris. About why we can't go over there."

"I want to see my cousins," Celine said.

"If it's toxic for you, if she's poison, why did you go to the café to talk to her?" Kristal said. "Look what it's done to you."

Philip's own plate was untouched. He stood, his chair banging against the window frame as he pushed away from the table. He carried the phone to a basket, put it inside, and dramatically wiped his palms together: *I wash my hands of this*. He returned to his seat and placed a cloth napkin on his lap. "You're right. That was a mistake. I'm not letting this take over my life," he said.

"I know you're just worried about your sister," Kristal said. Conciliatory now.

Philip turned and made a big face at Celine, waggling his eyebrows. "Daddy," she said, a small aristocrat trying not to collapse into giggles, daintily covering her mouth.

"Why don't we try to go over there? Maybe she's not as toxic anymore. For you." Kristal went to the sink for a cloth, wet it, and began to wipe Celine's face.

Philip watched as Celine tolerated this. She had never been a difficult child. Never stubborn, never fighting. Kristal told people that although she'd become a lawyer, she had never been stubborn nor particularly argumentative, and she believed it was a capacity for calm and self-control that led to success, not fiery blazes of inspiration. And indeed she was successful—enough to have been featured in a local glossy, enough to have become senior associate very quickly. "You're a little obsessed about the handsome person Sheryl saw with Francine, but I think you actually seem okay. Maybe your sister really doesn't rattle your cage that much anymore," she said.

Philip winced at the memory of arguments between him and Kristal in which he, fiery and ablaze, had ranted that phrase. *Rattle my cage*. It was his mother's phrase, transferred to him like the seed of an invasive plant. "Maybe you're right," he said. Maybe it was time to let it all go. But in spite of himself, he glanced over at the phone in its basket.

21

PHILIP, HIGH SCHOOL.

When he came back from Perth, Philip went immediately to his room and lay on his twin mattress, staring at the white popcorn ceiling. He felt confused and betrayed. He clenched his fists and tried to pray. He loved the dramatic verses in the Bible like *My God! My God! Why have you forsaken me?* and he thought about these now. Francine's actions with Howie were a message to him. A dismemberment, an act of severance, Philip thought. What she had done was not about either her or Howie, but instead about him, him, *Philip.* He remembered how, when he and Francine were small children, she would sometimes lick his portion of food to pollute it—not because she wanted it, but because he did. This wasn't exactly like that, though: he didn't *want* Howie. He wanted God. He wanted God, so Francine had to desecrate Him. And she probably wasn't even aware of what she was doing.

("I love you, you idiot," she was always telling him. Telling him and snarling.)

He lay there, clenching his fists, then got up to put on music—*emo*, his sister called it, derisive. He masturbated once, twice, tugging on his penis and then pulling on it so fast his hand and dick blurred into a fleshy beige smear as he thought nothing, just stroked until he exploded. The relief was only temporary. He wanted to cry. If she didn't return by six or seven on Saturday, he decided, he'd tell on her. He'd go to the dim woodshop and tell his father, who'd look up from his small drills and needles, his eyes obscured by the lenses of his goggles, and sigh. And together they'd keep the knowledge from his mother for a little while, until she sensed that they were hiding something and drew it out of them. Francine wouldn't even know that it was Philip who'd told on her.

Now there were tears in his eyes—just enough to wet them but not enough to collect into a droplet and fall.

The front door opened. What followed were the familiar sounds of his adolescence: his mother's alto voice, then his sister's alto voice, a cupboard door slamming, the fridge door sucking open and closed. "Where have you been?" his mother was saying when Philip came down to meet them at the table. Philip watched his sister drink wine; he watched her lie; he could hear everything in the merest wobble of her voice. Victoria launched into her usual lecture: what men were capable of, why a woman had an obligation to be careful. Philip found himself nodding, and Francine saw this and fled, stomping up the stairs. He sat at the table while his mother finished her glass. Music blasted from above. The opening track from a CD by Hole. His mother winced, swallowed more wine. "She thinks she invented teen angst," she said.

"I don't think she thinks that," Philip replied. No matter what he said, he would betray one of them.

AFTER A FEW minutes, Philip followed Francine upstairs and stood outside her door. He could hear her playing that doll parts song by Hole. Then there was a moment of silence followed by the sounds of that Nirvana CD with the naked baby on the cover. She was nostalgic for the world from just a few years earlier, when they'd been too young for grunge. Philip frowned. The grunge bands were nothing but nostalgia themselves, for a less corporate age, for punk rock and hippies and LSD. Aggressive guitar-slammed chords rattled her closed door like a wind. He knocked. No answer.

He knocked again. Knocked and tried the knob.

"What?" Her voice was hoarse.

"Can I come in?"

Heavy sigh. "Fine."

Francine was sprawled on her bed, surrounded by her stuffed Paddington bear, her stuffed bear Abraham, two unnamed stuffed koala bears and her stuffed rabbit, which was the size of a small child. Her t-shirt looked wet or grease-stained. No makeup, as usual, but her freckles seemed more pronounced than normal. Maybe it was because she was flushed. On the desk, her boom box blared that angry music. Those old grunge rockers loved imagery of dolls going bad, rusty, creepy instead of innocent. Barbies melting. There was no melting doll in Francine's room, but Philip imagined one there. A bald-headed doll with Sharpie-blacked-out eyes staring at him.

"Are you okay?" he asked. Although it was he who needed sympathy. He who needed someone to love him and tell him that there was a God after all.

"I dunno."

She looked at him with red eyes. He couldn't remember the last time he'd seen her cry.

"I, oh, God, don't tell Mom," she said. "Don't tell her anything. Please, Philip."

"I won't tell her," he said, and the cool ocean water of her confession came lapping at him. They could do this together.

"Thanks, Fip."

The window was open. Little licking gusts of air pushed the curtain out before sucking it back in, flesh draped over a rib cage. He wanted her to say more. He waited for her to say more. At last, he said, "Don't tell her what?"

Francine looked at him. It was a measured look, calculating.

"I had sex with—I think I'm in love with someone."

"Oh."

"Yeah, and—"

He waited.

"I don't know if he's a good guy, you know? I thought I loved him . . ."

"Who is he?" Philip said.

"Don't pretend you're going to be tough about this and beat him up or something."

"I wouldn't." He found he could barely speak. A spark of anger rushed in to replace the calm he'd felt a moment ago.

"I loved him. But I don't know exactly what he wants from me. We're—we're in different spaces in our lives."

How dare she talk like this, as if she were years older than him. "You think I don't understand," he said.

"You don't understand. No one does."

"Francine, I'm not as innocent as you think."

She looked at him dubiously. "Don't be angry. I hate when you get like this."

"Like what?"

"I dunno. So prim."

"Screw you."

"Don't, Fip, I can't take it right now. I can't." Suddenly she was sobbing. She pulled up her shirt to wipe away snotty tears. "Even if he has feelings for me, he lives so far away I can't possibly . . ." Her chest was heaving.

"I know more about all of this than you think I do."

"You're right. I'm sorry—" She looked at him. "I know I haven't been there for you."

It hadn't been so long ago that Philip had felt the presence of God swooping through the leaves of the tree outside his bedroom window. How could he live now in a world so empty of meaning? Her condescension was unbearable.

"You need to be careful," he said icily.

Her eyes turned mean again, like lenses that had just been capped. "Okay. We're done here," she said.

He left Francine's room and grabbed the cordless phone from his parents' bedroom. He took it to his own room, and dialled the number in Perth. Didn't Howie know that his sister was underage, didn't he know what was right and what was wrong? And even if she wasn't underage—was seventeen-nearly-eighteen underage?—this was wrong, it was adultery. Even a non-believer knew that. Philip knew. *I* know, and I'm just a kid, he'd cry at the phone.

No one answered. Okay. He called again; no answer. So Howie was a coward, too. In the silence after he put down the phone, Philip could faintly hear quieter music, sadder music— Radiohead—from Francine's room.

ON SUNDAY MORNING Philip rose early and dressed carefully. He wrote a note saying he was going fishing a few hours north with some youth group friends. It was still dark when he shut the front door, his parents sleeping, Francine asleep with her bears. At the gas station he pumped gas under floodlights. Trucks with their giant grilles took up the vista of his rear-view mirror. Pairs of white lights, pairs of red lights, his music with its companionable sweetness, its longing. *So emo*—as if that were a bad thing. Here was an event: dawn cracking.

It was fully light by the time he reached Perth and realized that Howie's house would be empty because the pastor was at church. He parked his car near the churchyard and walked up a grassy hill wedged with crumbling stone steps towards the building, from which came a hymn wrapped in voices and tremulous organ chords. The music hummed through his body, travelling up from the soles of his feet.

He stole into the small sanctuary and sat at the back. Howie was at the pulpit, wearing a white robe, an embroidered sash over either shoulder. The parishioners were mostly old white people, although Philip thought he could hear a baby whimper. But that might have been any sound in this echoing place.

"Brothers and sisters," Howie said. "Let's stand for the final benediction."

Philip stood, and that is when Howie saw him. He looked as though some shadowy part of him had slipped away from his body and collapsed beside him. Philip watched as he tried to pull on a smile, in the way one tries to pull on clothes in a dream where you're caught naked. Howie said something about the Father, the Son, the Holy Spirit. May the Lord keep you, may the Lord bless you, amen. Philip sang loudly along to this series of amens, a sheep in another man's pasture.

But Philip was no sheep, not anymore. To feel that another man was afraid, was in your power. In your hands. In Philip's hands, which were large enough to palm a basketball. The congregation was singing, and Philip was perhaps going to commit murder—with his hands!

The moment felt so real—how rarely he'd felt this vividly alive.

Now Howie was walking down the aisle and out of the church, and people filed out behind him to be blessed with a handshake and a kind word. It was easy to seem kind for the sake of your charm; it cost you nothing and rewarded you with much. But Philip knew that none of this was true kindness, which was hidden and secret and even terrifying, like the love of God. Philip allowed people to go ahead of him, positioning himself at the end of the line. Howie, he saw with new clarity, was attractive in a big-eyed, low-voiced, goofball kind of way.

"Philip," Howie said, betraying nothing. He was charming and looked at Philip lovingly. "It's wonderful to see you. You came all this way?"

"I have a car. It's no big deal." But he knew it must look to Howie as it did to him: like a very big deal. There were still a few people talking under the canopy of trees, another few slowly moseying to cars. The organist let out a sudden blast of music.

"Well, since you are here," Howie said, "do you want to grab coffee or lunch?"

"I don't want to interfere with your plans."

"My plans are to spend some time with you and then to take a long, untroubled nap."

"Untroubled."

"It's always a relief to have finished the Sunday morning duties."

"Right." Philip narrowed his eyes. "You are otherwise untroubled." He felt a current pass between them. Howie knew that he knew, but they were both going to keep pretending.

"I'm adjusting to a new routine, but it's nice to have a smaller church and a smaller life."

"We've hardly noticed you're gone," Philip said.

Howie tilted his head.

A breeze forced its way between them and the elderly organist, wearing thick glasses and very short white hair, bounded out the door. "That's Sunday for one more week!" the person said, their voice an alto or a tenor, ungendered like an angel.

"That's Sunday. See you later, Gene." Or Jean. Howie clapped Gene/Jean on the back, and Philip nodded, and the organist left them alone in front of the empty church. A thought crept over him: probably Howie wished he, Philip, was Francine so they could desecrate this space together, fucking on a pew, on an altar. And why not, if there was no God but lust?

"So," Howie said.

"You know, Pastor Howie," Philip said, channelling the tough guys he'd seen on TV cop shows. "You know when you sometimes feel like you did something wrong, but no one knows that you did? You think you got away with it? Some real sin, you know? Something really bad?"

"Okay, Philip, look."

"Yes?"

Howie sighed. He had the same exasperated way with a sigh that Francine did. "What did your sister tell you?"

"Nothing," Philip said. He was suddenly exhausted from the early morning, the drive, and now he felt that he might cry. How quickly he was losing the upper hand. "What do you mean?"

"I know that you two look out for each other."

"I look out for her."

"She looks out for you, too," Howie said.

Philip snorted. Some shadow of Howie again slipped away, drooped and fell.

"I want you to stay away from my sister."

Howie coughed loudly. "I live five hours away from your family. Maybe it's you who should stay away from me?"

Now Philip's bottom lip trembled. "We'll stay away. Don't speak to my sister anymore if you want to keep living this charade."

"This is not what you think. I don't know what you think you're getting at."

"Do you even believe in God?"

In later years, Philip would try to peel away all his anguish from this scene so that he could try to understand what Howie, this man, was going through. Later he would think: Howie had been young, just thirty-two, thirty-three—in his Jesus year, probably feeling broken-down and messianic.

Did I want to have sex with him? he would ask his therapist, would ask Kristal. But he knew that what he felt hadn't been lust; it was something bigger and more terrible. He had wanted his body to be broken open, his mind to loosen. He and Francine were both in love with Howie. And later, that was the rumour that would move as fast as spirit through every Presbyterian community in southern Ontario, driving Howie away, farther away than Perth, somewhere the spirits wouldn't reach him.

"Of course I believe in God," Howie said then. And his look at Philip was so full of pity. "I'm trying my best to be a good man."

22

—

FRANCINE, HIGH SCHOOL.

If Philip arrived home late, he was not interrogated, because this was what the world was for boys. But when Francine hassled her mother about misogyny—something she had started to do that year, and would do even more in the years to come—her mother flatly refused to acknowledge it. Women were asking for trouble. Men had certain qualities women naturally did not have.

"You're a woman," Francine said. "How can you say that? Don't you have rights?"

"My rights entitle me to have these opinions," her mother said. Or: "Don't be hysterical, Francine."

Francine hadn't even noticed that Philip had left the house that Sunday after she'd returned from visiting Howie. She spent most of the day lying amid her stuffed animals, mascara-streaked, listening to Fiona Apple, whose throaty, warbling voice sounded like sex. All lyrics were sex, were climax, and this was bliss, Francine thought, which was why she was crying. Bliss was more than any person could bear for long. Her skin in many places was raw, and she ran her finger along it, thought of Howie's voice, his mouth, the frightening hood of penis and its winking eye. His small kind words. I'm scared, she'd said to him only short days ago. Do you want to stop? No, she'd said. I want to be scared. Scare me, scare me, fuck me.

She was not yet thinking that the relationship could end. Instead, she believed a number of futures were possible. That she'd move in with Howie; that he'd leave his wife for good; that he'd leave the church and they'd be together. People did things like this. It was the nineties, and nobody had to live by rules they didn't believe in.

She rose from the bed and walked around her room. She ate a piece of fruit she'd taken upstairs from the kitchen. She admired her reflection in the mirror over her dresser. Her long lashes, her fine nose and chin, her small mouth. She picked up CD cases from her loose pile, wishing now that she had the one Howie had been playing; she wanted that music to blast over her body, she wanted it to cry in her ear as he had. What a thing for a man to give himself to a woman, to offer her his vulnerability and trust, to say, Yes, I'm sorry, I'm sorry, I love you. He'd said he'd loved her, hadn't he?

She checked the lock on her door again, returned to bed, and put her hand into her panties, just to hold it there, something to relieve the pressure of her wanting, the pressure of having been released from her wanting.

—

THE NEXT MORNING, a Monday, she and Philip drove to school together. He refused to look at her.

"I really can't believe you," he said.

"You can't understand me," she said. "Because I live on another plane of existence. I'm floating here, and you think you're floating too. You aren't."

"What?"

"Oh, don't worry," she said. "I'm joking." But she was shaky, as if she had gone too long between meals or without sleep. Time was passing oddly, and whenever she checked a clock, hours had passed in which all she could remember was lying down, barrelling into her own thoughts, tunnelling into the future, into the past, into that moment when Howie had touched her, the first moment he'd touched her.

"Francine?"

"Don't worry. It's just love. People fall in love, Philip!"

"You aren't acting normal." Instead of turning toward the school, he drove straight through an intersection, and then veered suddenly to the side of the road where there was almost no shoulder.

"What the hell, Fip."

"I know you better than anyone else." His keys, still in the ignition, dangled with several dog tag–style chains. His face seemed as young as a small boy's, and Francine felt the loss of his boyhood as though it were a weight rushing towards her gut, like a demolition ball. "And this version of you scares me. I don't know whether to be mad at you or worried about you."

"Why would you be mad?"

Cars were rushing around them. Someone honked loudly, flipped them an angry finger.

"Okay," he said, barely turning to check the road before twisting the car around in a violent U-turn. "Okay."

"Okay, what? Philip, why would you be mad?"

"I guess there's no reason at all why I'd be angry with you, huh?"

She frowned at him sympathetically—and saw him see her sympathy and recoil from it. "I don't know," she said. "I really, really don't."

"You never think of other people's feelings. You think you can do anything you want."

The demolition ball rested on her gut.

When Philip parked the car at school, she refused to get out right away, and he threw his keys at her. They knocked into her teeth, leaving a cut on her mouth, which she touched with her finger. He had left her there with his car, his keys, and she thought, wildly, of driving to Howie's. But she wasn't about to prove Philip's point about her, so eventually she picked up her backpack, locked the car and entered the school.

High school, as usual, was a stew of rumours. At lunchtime, a boy came up to Francine and told her he'd heard she'd lost her virginity to a teacher. An old guy. The girls she sat with, nose-ringed and eyeliner-smeared, looked up, casually interested. "What's virginity?" she said, affecting cool with her eyes half-closed. The boy was not put off by this. He made a circle of his thumb and finger and stuffed another finger into the hole and thrust it in and out. "Impressive," Francine said, hoping that her embarrassment had not made her skin splotchy.

"Get lost already," said one of her girlfriends.

The boy did leave, this boy with his thin dusting of moustache, and returned to a table full of other boys who erupted into mean laughter and applause.

"Who needs these people," Francine said.

"Seriously," said another of her friends.

After school she confronted Philip, and he denied saying a word about her to anyone.

"But *I* didn't tell anyone," she said.

"You must have."

"I didn't." She clutched her bag as he drove. "You hurt me earlier," she said quietly.

But Philip just stared hard at the road. He didn't talk to her again for months.

23

FRANCINE, PRESENT.

Maggie complimented Francine on her furniture, her paint colour, her plants. It was days like this—dreary January, wet, grey, salt ringing the streets, slush hardening into dirt—that made a person, Maggie said, long for the desert. Francine's boys were home from school, and the house was alight with their constant motion. Simon had turned a cardboard box into an ersatz computer and was pretending to type so quickly that he seemed a pianist. Red was sitting on the floor and had arranged blocks, bits of fencing from a farm set, train tracks, and animals in a complicated game. Simon looked up from time to time to gaze longingly at his brother's toys, and then sighed and turned back to his typing, as though at the prospect of many hours of work.

"If I was the predator when I was seventeen and eighteen," Francine said to Maggie, "then I can't be the predator now."

"You weren't the predator then, you dummy. Don't go back there."

"I ruined his life," Francine said. "I ruined Howie's life."

"There are support groups for this kind of shit, you know. There are twelve-step programs." Maggie sounded breathless with anxiety. "Jesus. Just get a hold of yourself. And don't tell anybody else. No one."

Francine mixed muffin batter in a metal bowl. "I have this feeling of foreboding." She lifted a spatula-sized hunk of batter into the muffin tin, one cup at a time. "I feel like someone is watching me."

"That's your conscience, babe," Maggie said. She was sitting at the high breakfast bar, and now she blew on her hot tea.

"Want to lick this?" Francine said, and handed Maggie the spatula. Maggie had her curls pulled into a bun, and her face looked plump and young. "It's not my conscience. What am I doing wrong? I know it looks bad. I know people will judge it, but why is it wrong?"

"He was a child when you met."

"He was sixteen when we met."

"A child."

"But who does this harm?"

"It harms him. And Jamie. And your kids, probably."

"My kids?" Francine said, heat from the stove or from inside her body rising to her face. She slammed the muffin tray into the oven. "I'll give you Jamie. But that's private and that's our marriage," she whispered, looking over at Simon and Red on the floor in the living room, lifting a toy train, lifting a toy plane, making the sounds of engines.

"So you don't feel guilty?" Maggie said.

"Do you feel guilty about your relationships?"

"No."

"Maggie, please." Francine turned her head away to look out the kitchen window. The house next door was rented by students, scattered through the rooms and anonymous as insects. "I need you to hear me. I know what's right and wrong and I'm not an idiot and I don't need a lecture."

"But you can't keep—"

"I look at my life, and I think that ever since I was a girl, and now that I'm a woman, a wife, a mother, there are grooves in place for me. Like one of those toy stick-figure hockey games where the players can only move within the small path cut out for them on the plywood surface, but that's it. Back and forth, a little wiggle. I mean, who is my life for? The family, monogamy, right? As if I'm just an essential atom in this system, and this system needs to be upheld."

"Right. But just because the system is a problem doesn't mean that people aren't real within it, or that they can't be hurt."

"I know that. Obviously, I know that."

"Don't get upset with me. I'm just worried about you because I love you."

The student house had eavestroughs that had been overfilled with wet leaves all autumn, and now dangled with heavy icicles. Everything in the everyday world required so much upkeep. To be in love, though, Francine thought—to feel desperate—that was the only true thing. "I realized something this week," she told Maggie. "I realized why I'm obsessed with Mary and the 'do not touch me' passage."

"Oh, that's interesting. Why?"

"Remember when Jesus recognizes Mary and says her name? On the one hand, I think you can live your ordinary duty-bound life, and once in a while something comes along to shake it . . . maybe you hold your child for the first time; it doesn't have to be sex. You feel that real connection."

"Right."

"Someone sees you. Wants you. Knows your name."

Maggie put the spatula down on the counter. "You're chasing the real thing."

"Yes." As Francine spoke, she felt the world come into focus, the edges sharpening—it was her and Maggie now. Really there, together.

"You get that from sex?" asked Maggie.

"Sometimes I do."

"He's so young, though, babe. There's a power dynamic. You were his *teacher*."

"I know."

"You look a little wrecked."

"I do?"

"You can't keep going like this."

"I have a fantasy of taking him in and introducing him to Jamie and making us polyamorous. He'd hang out with us, and we'd know him."

"Domesticating the fantasy. Won't work. You can't just chase your id's desires and then expect to have a civilization. Sometimes eros is just one step away from Thanatos," Maggie said.

"You sound like a graduate student from 1983," said Francine.

Maggie laughed. "You still need to tell yourself the truth."

"What's the truth?"

"You're using him to feel something about what happened long ago. Maybe to forgive yourself?"

A week ago, Francine had finally received a text from Howie. It had that same old preacherly tone: *This is Francine? I'm in town for a few days, and I would be happy to meet for a coffee.* This, she decided, she could not tell Maggie.

"No, no, no!" Red shrieked and threw a toy at Simon's cheek. Simon put his hand to his face and turned calmly, his eyes filling, to look at Francine. He held his cheek and stared at her until she ran over to hold him in her lap. "He did it," Red said. "It was him."

"But I saw you," Francine said. "I saw you throw a train car at your brother."

"It was him," Red said.

Francine held Simon, shushing and rocking, her son so big that his legs dangled over her bent knees.

"Mommy," Red said, pleading. And so she gathered him into her lap, too.

24

FRANCINE, PRESENT.

Francine was on her way to Alexander's house later that week when Howie finally texted her a time, a place to meet. It had to be that morning, he wrote; he had a flight to catch. There was no resisting, thought Francine, though what she really wanted was not Howie but Alexander and his body, his bed, his mercy on her. She needed it in the way a person needs a good drug.

You're a potion, she'd murmured to Alexander the last time they were together. His arms were long and lean, with small round muscles around the shoulder, across the bicep, a little cut of a muscle where his tricep throbbed as he braced himself over her.

They would be caught soon. She could feel it. And before that happened, she wanted to fuck and to fuck, and to be fucked, until she was no person at all.

"We're both adults," he'd said, leaning in to kiss her. "Nothing bad will happen." He put his erection into the wet, numb, overwhelmed meat of her cunt, rubbed it over her clit, and she gasped. "God, I love it when you do that," he said. "I live to make you do that."

"Some people are just compatible," she had told Maggie, who was tiring of her protestations, who wore judgment on her face like a too-tight mask pulling her expression into primness.

"Imagine, some people never have sex for their entire lives," Maggie said.

Sometimes, Francine felt how young he was. She'd wake from a post-coital nap to see Alexander hunched over his phone, sending idiotic memes to someone. His Twitter feed lacked insight. He would get worked up over how badly he'd done on a paper, and she'd read it, only to find it riddled with stupidity, with comments about humankind from the beginning of time cribbed from Merriam-Webster definitions.

Today, she'd have to stand him up. She imagined him hard with anticipation, only to turn soft and slump, maybe wondering where she was. She imagined him small, as helpless as somebody's son. I was somebody's daughter, she thought then, and the pain of it pricked at her like shards of ice.

It was about to rain: the sky was a concrete slab. She texted her details to Howie and was on her way to yet another coffee shop—that other, earlier coffee shop frozen in time inside her, a spot where she'd go and meet her young childish body, her small sexy body, her face a gaping maw of need. Yes, she was on her way. She was shaking. Recently, she had missed so many meals. At a red light, she caught a glimpse of her reflection in the rear-view mirror. Fanning wrinkles around each eye, a vertical slice of nose between them, a big freckle on her lip.

She felt a surge of worry that, she knew, could only be remedied by her husband. She called him. "Hey," Jamie said, so steady and comforting, always full of cheer. The sounds of their own coffee shop swirled in the background. Spray, hiss, burst of laughter. "What's up?"

She had no ready pretense for the call, so she asked if he'd received an email they were expecting from Simon's teacher. The two of them talked aimlessly about this until Jamie told her he would have to address it when he got home. "There's a line at the counter," he said.

"Of course, of course," she said, pressing the red button on the dash to end the call.

She parked and held the wheel, making herself breathe. Was Howie inside already, waiting for her? He must be fifty by now, a distinguished older man or a schlub. Oh my god, she whispered. At seventeen, at eighteen, when he'd abandoned her, what wouldn't she have done to know that her life would be this one, now?

Again she looked in the mirror, and fixed up her eyeliner and the shine on her lips. Soon she would get out of the car. Soon, she would get out of the car. Soon, she would. Soon, soon.

25

PHILIP, UNIVERSITY.

In the newly built student centre on campus, and in the basement corridors outside lecture halls, there were tents and sleeping bags and piles of backpacks alongside a variety of instruments—guitars and djembes, mostly. At least one bearded or (white) dreadlocked student was always sitting in the encampment. Flyers were pasted onto bulletin boards and walls; poorly painted signs littered the campus; there were endless op-eds in the student paper: all protesting the war in Iraq.

Philip couldn't stand any of it. Not that he was pro-war. He wasn't a fascist; he didn't fetishize military power. But his school was in Canada, these were Canadian kids, and the conflict in Iraq was an American war. In the days after the 9/11 attacks he'd sat in his Canadian literature class listening to a woman—a mature student in her thirties—talk about how the military had no choice but to strike back. Someone else had been crying about the need for peace, and then ranting, tearfully, about hate crimes against Muslims. The professor, a man whose glasses were always askew and whose sweaters had the biggest sleeves Philip had ever seen pooling around his wrists, tried in vain to turn the class back to Emily Carr, to Leonard Cohen.

How did his classmates know so much about what to believe politically? Philip felt their protest was pure performance, pure theatre—but that turned out to be a political stance too, and now they were all supposed to believe they lived in a time beyond irony. Just when he'd begun to understand what was meant by irony! A friend in the dorms who had been planning to go to the WTO protests talked at him for hours about corporate abuses: did he know, for example, that a corporation was considered a person?

"In Canada, too?" Philip asked.

"It doesn't *matter*, man. We're de facto Americans."

Philip had tried to join the Inter-Varsity Fellowship, but those friends, too, made their beliefs known by wearing t-shirts emblazoned with religious quotes or praying in one of the university's cafeterias before meals, hands clasped and head bowed. Also, he saw now, a performance. When he stood to sing and clap with the others—for songs he had loved when Howie led them—he felt only grief and doubt and unease. He knew the Inter-Varsity leaders would tell him to hold fast, to wait it out, this leakage of his faith. But they, like him, were only twenty years old. He tried to go to faith rallies on the weekend; he wanted to rally his belief, he wanted God back, he wanted Jordan, he wanted Howie. He wanted to stand among that crowd of people and feel so full of the spirit of God he didn't know that he himself existed anymore, let alone that he was mortal, let alone that he was sinful.

He wanted to collapse his boundaries inside that crowd. Instead, he felt only more grief, mounting grief. He found he wanted to put his fist through something. He couldn't go home, but he couldn't stay on campus, either. On the verge of dropping out, he went to visit Steven, who lived nearby in the city.

"Do you think maybe that you miss Francine?" his brother asked. Steven, recently out of the closet, had moved to Toronto, where he was bartending while he decided whether or not to go to med school or law school.

The mention of his sister's name. Philip felt an uncomfortable heat rise inside him. "I don't miss her, no."

"You've never been apart for this long, have you?"

"I guess not."

"Maybe it's having an effect on you that you don't see. She's a very powerful person."

This was a phrase their mother always used about Francine. "Funny that the women in our family are so powerful," Philip said. "So certain of themselves."

He dreaded seeing his sister at Christmas; she would have no patience for his floundering. And she would have a series of complicated reactions to the political situation, all of which were beyond his current imagining. After Steven had come out, Philip had briefly wondered whether he himself was gay—it seemed at least possible that he was bi—but he had neither the certainty nor the courage to experiment and find out. Instead he understood himself to be a person who let others lead him. A person with no opinions or preferences of his own.

Steven offered to make him a drink. "I'm getting pretty good at martinis," he said. But Philip could not think of a single cocktail by name.

"I usually drink beer," he said, though he didn't.

"I'm going to make us White Russians," Steven said. "The *Big Lebowski* special."

Watching Steven move around his galley kitchen like a real adult, Philip realized that his brother was right: he, Philip, might be angry with Francine—but he did miss her.

"Sometimes people depend on others, even if they'd rather not. Sometimes people even rely on the presence of their abusers to feel okay." Steven pulled things out of the fridge and freezer—a frosted bottle of Smirnoff, a half-litre of cream—while Philip struggled to know what to do with his hands. "Not that I'm saying you have an abuser. Not that I'm saying that. But people learn to desire whatever makes them feel at home."

"Is that true?"

"I don't know. Maybe the opposite is true!" Steven had always seemed warm and industrious, like their father, but there was something in his long-fingered elegance, his severe, thin nose, that made his resemblance to their mother in this moment feel uncanny. "When I used to watch the two of you fight, I would hate it because you fought exactly like Mom and Dad fight."

"But Mom and Dad don't fight."

Steven put down the bottle of Kahlúa and, holding the counter, looked at Philip with a very dramatic expression of surprise and amusement. "Mom and Dad's fights are the reason I rarely come home. I felt guilty, sometimes, for abandoning the two of you there."

"I have never once in my life seen Dad get angry. I can count on one hand the number of times I've seen Mom get mad."

Steven handed a glass to Philip. Condensation cooled and wet his skin.

"I feel for Mom, I really do, but the way she treats Dad is horrible," Steven said. "Just constantly snapping at him. He'd cough, gently, and she'd shout at him from the next room, shout his name. *How dare you cough in my house* was the subtext. I hated it. I couldn't wait to leave."

"And that reminds you of me and Fanny?"

"I'm not saying that Francine is so bad, or as bad as that. And anyone can see that the battle of wills between her and Mom is epic stuff. But there's a pattern there. I thought, I hoped even, that Mom and Dad would get divorced."

They moved into Steven's small living area—a bedroom and living room combined. Steven perched on the edge of the bed; Philip sank into a ratty armchair. The drink was mostly sweetness, mostly creaminess, with a warming bite of vodka.

"Delicious, right?"

Philip nodded.

"I want to tell you something," Steven said, "even though I don't think either of us should really know it. Or maybe I'm wrong about that. It doesn't feel like my story to tell, is what I'm saying, and honestly, I sometimes wish I didn't know. I wish Mom hadn't told me the way she did."

Alongside the warmth coursing through Philip came another feeling now, a bad feeling.

"I think Mom worked to not be like she was with me, with the two of you. To have better boundaries. She must have been in a particular stage of her life when I was growing up," Steven said.

The light outside had begun fading to night, and Philip clutched the drink, taking small sips, each making him wonder why his lips felt so dry.

"She could be really inappropriate," Steven continued. "I think she had met someone at work. That's what I gathered from listening to them fight. Anyhow, one day she came to my room and sat down on my bed and said, 'I need you to know what happened to me when I was a girl. I need you to know what the world is like, what people are capable of.'"

Steven's face became more and more shadowy as the sun set. Two squares of pale light shone through big bare windows to illuminate one side of his body while the other faded into an outline. Philip looked around in vain for a lamp that might be within reach.

"The abuse had gone on for years. A good friend of Grandpa's."

"Stop," Philip said, or thought he said into this dim, unfamiliar room.

26

FRANCINE, PRESENT.

F rancine pressed firmly with her thumb on the locking mech-
anism of her fob and listened as the car cheeped. Its lights
flashed on and then off. People cheat all the time, she thought,
and not everybody turns it into a delusion or a wound. People
cheat all the time and not everyone goes around acting like it's a
catastrophe. But she felt alone, just as she had at seventeen, and
filled with disdain for her family. Jamie and his kindness were no
cloak anymore.

At the counter of the coffee shop she ordered a double-
double and a donut. Maple crème. Why not treat herself? She
was thinking like a person in Vegas whose deeds will stay in
Vegas. Or like a person who knows she's about to drive off a
cliff. What a relief that would be. A world without her, where
her sons could be raised by a good and kind and steady person.

It was only after she'd purchased and received the coffee and donut that she permitted herself to look around the shop. It was filled with people in jeans and sweats, a family of five dropping crumbs all over one table, people wearing ball caps. There was a squealing baby in a messy high chair in one corner. How quaint. This felt to Francine like a return to an old scene—although she had changed, the scene had stayed the same all this time.

She saw him then. He might have been any white-haired man with large hands sitting at a corner table with a lidless coffee. A thin line of steam from his cup wisped into the air.

"There you are," she said.

"Oh, Turkey," he said. His face, when it broke into a smile, was as kind and lovely as it had ever been. Three, four lines around each side of his mouth. Bits of white hair in his beard, as if it were sugar-dusted.

The old longing rushed back at Francine, unstoppable—the longing to be of another era, to be Mary Magdalene herself. To be called out of the slumber of pettiness and sin into a world that was no longer a place of men who wanted to degrade and punish her, to closely watch over her or stone her to death, but a place of intellectual and spiritual intrigue. If she were Mary, following behind Jesus, she would watch his back. She would watch his shoulders, which would one day be stretched and pressed to a cross. She would watch as he walked in the hot desert sun, hands full of blessings, his robe soiled and dusty at his feet. She would be Mary, with her head covered, anonymous in the crowd until—as she'd hoped would happen—he turned around and beamed at her. His face breaking open. "Oh, Mary."

To be seen and known and not to be despised or ejected from the kingdom. Francine understood: Mary Magdalene hadn't known what to do with her feelings except to be always at Jesus's back, or at his feet, adoring, listening, soaking up his being. Later, after he'd been hung from the cross, she had wandered in the garden, not knowing where they had put her Lord. She had seen him suffer. And when in the garden he came up to her and said again, "Oh, Mary," another kind of eternity took on flesh, electric storms slicing the air.

Francine ached for a life like that, an ancient life not surveilled by the internet and by marriage, a world shot through with the eternal. As she sat there, across from Howie, the gift that was her thesis, the ideas she'd been working through, came back to her. Maybe she could still work it out, could finish it. Maybe she could turn away from this old scene at last and make it into the past, gone and over. Howie was her muse, even if he didn't know it. He had natural charisma, not abused for the purpose of acquiring power. He was able to see and to love. He was merciful.

"I wish I were more like you," she said now. "I don't seem to be capable of love the way you are. I remember how you were with others."

He took this in slowly, catching up to her thoughts. Francine saw that he was more tired than he'd been those years ago. "You wanted that from me," he said at last.

"I wanted what?"

"You wanted something that you thought I had."

"No," she said. "No."

He picked up his cardboard cup of coffee. She waited, holding her breath. How often in life, she thought, does one get to have a conversation like this? To pull away the curtain and tell the truth?

"What was it you wanted from me, then?"

"I was in love with you. I was too young, but I was in love."

He looked away from her.

"It was real. You can't tell me it wasn't," she said.

"You were a kid," he said. "I could only see it sometimes, but when I saw it I was horrified at what we'd done. You were a kid in my charge. I was supposed to be a mentor and a shepherd. I was supposed to show you how to live and to offer you a safe place."

"I felt safe with you. Always."

"You were so scared that first time. I hardly slept for a year. The insomnia, the guilt, I—I could see you were a kid and you were scared, and I did it anyway."

Something terrifying rushed towards her. It was time itself, maybe, come to push its force against the edges of her body.

"Are you okay?" he said.

"Yeah—I—"

"We don't have to talk about this, you know. It's long over. But I can see that you're not okay, and I know that's my fault. It's also my duty as a human being and as a Christian to receive the news of my guilt."

What a strange way of talking. His wrinkles had hardened into grooves around his eyes and eyebrows, around his mouth.

"You're still a Christian?" Francine said.

"Where else could I go with my sin and find mercy?"

"Couldn't it be, rather than sin, more like a mess of bad timing and strong feelings?" she said. "Couldn't it be that I was really in love with you and you loved me, too, and we were great together even though the timing was bad?"

"It was only two nights," he said. He looked her full in the eyes, finally, and she felt a charge pass between them. "I thought, you know, when you wanted to see me now, that you wanted to be angry on behalf of your younger self. Angry about this crime we committed together, this ability we had to tell ourselves a lie so that we could do what we wanted."

"The crime we committed together?"

"I mean the crime I committed. *My* crime. Of course."

"But couldn't it be true that people fall in love inconveniently sometimes? The only thing I'm angry about is that you shut me out without saying a word. Without saying a word or making a call or sending a note, not even goodbye. You froze me out. It broke my fucking heart. I lost years because of that."

Alexander, she knew, was across town in his attic room this very moment, waiting for her. And she wouldn't come. Howie was about to burst the bubble of that love, too—and maybe she should be glad for that. Maybe this was what she needed—good, hard medicine. She knew that she would soon start to cry. Next to her an older couple had stilled and were eavesdropping: she could feel their attention shift, could feel their ears perking up. This couple with their bad haircuts and puffy coats. Here was her moment of eternity in yet another coffee shop, with this couple as her witness. She turned and grinned at them, an evil grin.

"Francine," Howie said.

The couple moved over to another table. "It broke my fucking heart," she said.

"Francine, I was married. I was a minister, and I had a lapse of judgment because I didn't want to be an adult. You seemed to offer me another life, one in which there were no responsibilities, was nothing but pleasure, and the temptation was too great for me. It's a sad thing—I see it so clearly now—when an adult tries to take something for themselves from a child instead of taking responsibility for their heart and soul."

"It seems like we have very different interpretations of what happened," Francine said. She closed her eyes to test whether she could still conjure the piles of books, the crates of records, young Howie flipping a CD case open. "I can see you think I was abused and that I'm in denial. But if I could have had it my way, no one would have guessed what had happened, and spread rumours about us. We'd still be together now."

"Your brother came to see me, you know."

"What?"

"Philip came to see me."

"What, recently?"

"No, back then. Right after the first night we spent together."

"What?" Francine tried to remember that day when she'd returned home and lay on her bed, weeping from every orifice. Listening to Hole, she thought, laughing at herself ruefully.

"I thought he was threatening to kill me if I touched you again. It was such a mess. I thought it would be better if we just let it end. I know I didn't tell you what I was planning, but—"

"So you broke it off because of Philip? I'm going to kill him."

"Don't blame him."

"Are you serious? He's still mad at me. He's been mad at me for years. He thinks I took his faith away. He's been attacking me for years. Honestly, I—now I don't know what—what happened, I—I can't believe this."

"He was right to be angry with me. Not with you. With me."

"How did he know?"

"He said he followed you in his car. He followed your buses and your train. He said he knew where you were headed anyway."

Now time rushed madly at her, pulled the air out of her lungs and dizzied her.

Howie reached for her hand. His large hand holding her small one. "You have a life," he said. "This is what I want to tell you."

Now he seemed to think he could bless her. She had allowed his hand to hold her hand. She felt the power of his touch—his crazy big hands—shoot through her, a current in each finger. He rubbed his thumb over her knuckles. Didn't he know that was erotic? "You have a husband who loves you, you have two children, two sweet sons who need you."

"I don't want it," she said. She reminded herself to speak quietly so that she didn't frighten him away.

"You shouldn't say that."

"I'm like a horse, you know. A wild horse that wants to run, and can tolerate the bindings for a while, and—"

"That's a very self-flattering image," he smiled at her. So kind.

"So it is," she said. "Won't you flatter me? Tell me that I was the one for you. Tell me that you only wish what I wished. That you wish we could have been the right ages for each other."

"If we'd been the same age you wouldn't have loved me. You wanted to be able to worship me." He was still holding her hand. "We were made for community and for worship. We were made for the good love of God."

"We were made," she said. Piety was a wall she wanted to blast through. "To fucking lose our minds for love once or twice in our lives."

"No one can live that way for long. How can that be what we're made for?" He released her hand. "I have to go. I think it's better if I go. You're a good person, Francine. We shared something and I am glad to see you thriving."

Thriving? "Don't go," she said.

He stood and picked up his parka from the back of the seat. She stood, too, and followed him to the door. The cold air outside was cleansing. "It was good to see you," he said. "I mean that from the bottom of my heart." He opened his arms and leaned in to hug her goodbye. She fell against his body, and he wrapped his arms around her. No one gave them a second glance. They were just two adults sharing an embrace.

"Couldn't we do this instead?" she said into his cheek. "Let's just find somewhere to be together. Just for today. Just for this afternoon, we could be together."

"I've made vows."

"You made promises to me, too. You never kept them."

"That wasn't real," he said, stepping back.

As if he could turn reality into a dream or a fantasy with the snap of his finger. "It *was* real," Francine said. She grabbed his hand again. "It's the only real thing and you're a coward."

"Maybe I am. Maybe I'm a coward."

"Please," she said. "Please don't go." But he patted her gently on the shoulder, as though filled with a spiritual kind of pity.

FRANCINE DROVE TO Alexander's apartment, feeling as though she were swimming in heavy, deep water. She raced across town through the traffic, parked, badly, in a space in front of his building, and ran up the outside stairs. She was drowning in her heavy clothes. She pushed his buzzer hard with her thumb. Held it down and pushed it again. Finally the door clicked open. She rushed the indoor stairs, too, and when Alexander opened his door for her, she entered and pushed it closed, locked each of the latches and the padlock and the grooved nub on the knob, and pulled the chain closed too. Adrenaline coursed through her.

"Are you okay? You're like two hours late."

She took off her coat first, then her boots, then pulled off each sock as tenderly as one removes the socks of a small, tearful child. Touched her long, elegant feet, aware of their faint smell of her boots' leather and sweat. She pulled her sweater up over her head. "I have too many clothes on," she said.

Alexander laughed and moved to kiss her. This kiss, she took; she pulled his body to her body and took his kiss as one takes communion. She knew now that this was a kind of divine ritual. And she knew that if she left this apartment, she'd never come back. "You're so handsome," she said.

"Are you drunk?" he said. "Did you drive drunk?"

She pulled her shirt off, so that she was wearing only her jeans and her bra, a nice bra she'd bought for the sake of this affair. Blush pink and lacy, so that her nipples peeping out from the lacy bits were coyly camouflaged. He kissed her again, putting his smooth hands on her, flicking her nipples with his thumbs.

"No," she said, suddenly sure of herself. "I don't want to right now."

"Okay," he said. Boys these days were taught about consent.

"I need to talk to you." She grabbed her t-shirt from the pile where she'd dropped it and put it on again. "Maybe there will be time for fucking after that."

She looked around the room with its items that would soon pop out of her existence. His bookshelf with all his books—his Camus, his Sartre, his Nietzsche, his Said, his collected works of Shakespeare, his D. H. Lawrence, the collection of a well-educated college boy—and its tchotchkes from Europe, from his mother, from Lebanon. Figurines carved of what looked like ebony or jade.

"Don't say 'fucking' like that."

"I thought you liked it," she said.

He frowned, and she saw how he looked like a small boy when he did that with his mouth. At his age, his body was still pumped full of collagen, which was why his skin was so smooth. He'd never suffered acne, not a single pock on his cheeks or chin. "I don't," he said.

"Okay. I'm sorry." His couch, she knew from experience, was as uncomfortable as it looked. "Tell me that you didn't come back here so you'd be close to me. Tell me you didn't leave Queen's for me." She sat on the couch, and its arm dug into her back.

"I didn't," he said.

"Why did you come back here, then?"

It was a sinkhole, this city. Certainly for him. And here she was, too, thirty-six and having done nothing at all. Why had she done nothing with her life?

"I did come back here for you," he said. A complete, instantaneous reversal. "I've been trying to tell you that I want to be with you. I want to be with you."

"I'm doing this to you," she said.

"Why can't we just be together? We're so happy when we're together."

"Because you're young and I'm old. Because if we announced ourselves to the world we'd be shunned. There would be no being together."

"We could move to another country."

"I'll get too old eventually and you won't want to be with me."

"That's lame. Older men stay with younger women all the time. Let me be the pretty one."

"Oh, no." He was pleading with her exactly as she had pleaded with Howie.

"What?"

"I have children, Alex. I can't leave my kids."

She looked out of his window to the street so that he wouldn't see her tearing up. It was safe and anonymous here. A woman three storeys below walked her small white dog, her breath cloudy in the cold air. How many times had she and Alexander been together now, in this room? *I'm not ready to see it*, she protested. To whom?

"I just saw—I just—do you remember I told you about that older man I had an affair with?"

"You just saw him?"

"I just saw him. Just now," she said. Her arms and legs suddenly felt thin, although she knew they weren't—as if the stress were causing her bones to push through layers of flesh.

"Did you have sex with him?"

"No," she said. "Sit down."

"I don't want to sit."

She felt as if she were a teacher again. She had a sudden vision of herself as his initiator into the world of women. She saw that there was no appeal for him in a girl—not unless that girl was wise and he could test his power with her. "I'm jealous, too," she said. "I don't want to lose you, either." But her words were unconvincing to her own ears. How easily love left. She hated her voice, how it sounded so maternal and calm.

"Okay, I'll fuck you now," he said, and he sat on the couch beside her. He pulled her shirt off. *Okay*, she said, and he unclipped her bra, moving roughly through the things he loved to do to her. She couldn't bear his show of rage, but felt a duty to receive it. It was what she deserved. The stupid things a person said to another person when they were alone together. Where else could you find such honesty? Only among children and the mad. Children, the mad, and here—with lovers out of control. She was the one who pulled off her pants but when he put his palm over the mound of her vulva, she squirmed away. "I don't have the stomach for this anymore," she said, whispering. The look on his face was that of a starved animal. He a tiger, she the hanks, the flanks, the meat and bones. Like he was about to snarl and snap. She resigned herself to the possibility that he would, but instead he sat up and stared out that same window where she had stared earlier, now fogged with their breath.

"I had something I wanted to tell you, I needed to tell you," she said.

"You don't get to do this," he said.

She got up and walked into his bedroom and stared at the bed, at the big glass door to the balcony. Pressed against this window, bent over that ledge, tied to the bedposts, on the kitchen counter: how could she have?

"You can't just do this," he said.

She went out onto the balcony and sat on the patio chair. It was cold, and she began to shiver. It occurred to her that he could lock her out there. And what if he did: would she jump? Would she break the window?

"It's not right." He stood at the opening onto the balcony. Hot air fled the room behind him. She wanted to find her way back to what she'd felt at the cottage: that she was a young woman, he a man.

"You've read a bit of poetry," she reminded him.

"And I think I ought to follow my heart."

"You will find someone else," she said. "It only hurts right now."

"Did it fade with that guy? That older guy?"

"I'm married," she said, stupidly. Her whole life was a farce. Each of her decisions. "Do you ever get the feeling like the gods are just messing with us? Like the Greek gods messed with the human world?"

"All the time," he said, not looking at her.

She touched her hand to his, and he let her, let her touch his fingers. "What if we rewind everything and go back to the first time we kissed, the first time we touched, the first time you flirted with me, and we go through them all until they didn't happen?"

"You're my favourite teacher," he said, and looked right into her eyes.

27

FRANCINE, PRESENT.

F rancine had done the right thing at last. Yes, even though
the landing had been hard and winter a thing to endure.
She lay in bed next to Jamie, who lay next to his teetering pile of
biographies, always asleep before she was, exhausted by the work
of the café. She lay there and ran her tongue over her clean teeth,
touched herself idly, and tried to imagine what would come next.
She would go back to her Ph.D., that was the main thing. She
would finish it now, because she understood Mary in the garden, understood what she wanted to say. She imagined herself
in her pile of books as she drifted along to sleep—but as always,
Alexander appeared, at first as an awareness in her periphery and
then as a man standing in front of her. A man, not a boy; a man
with stubble on his face, wearied by heartbreak. *Ms. Nichols.*
A hiss. *I haven't told anyone.*

He would tell someone. There was no help for it. He would live for years and decades having seduced his teacher. He would fall in love. The beauties he would find, and then the one he would court and marry. Nobody knew what the world would think about these things in twenty years. She, meanwhile, could remember the smell of strawberries. Alexander putting them to his nose to inhale that intensity; she, several feet away, smelling them as though she had crawled into his body, was staring from his eyes as if from a mask. He in the small grocery store, unbearably handsome. If she went back to his apartment now, she could still have him. The temptation to do so was almost more than she could bear. But she would not go back.

She had once been a teacher who loved her students—and not as a punchline to a gossipy joke. She'd felt the real love of a mentor for a protegé, of an adult who wants the best for a child. There had been girls who came to her for advice and told her *no one listens to me.* Kids who stayed after school for help from her, who puzzled over the meaning of phrases in Shakespeare and Baldwin and Stoppard. They were privileged kids, yes, but they had felt alone, and she had helped them.

And she had experienced the same in her own education. Eli at the high school had mentored her, and nothing had happened between them. That was the way it was supposed to be. Eli had encouraged her to apply for a full-time position. Now the joke was on her: she thought she'd been on a path of pursuing her desires, but here she was: just another woman ruined by sex. An independent woman ruining her life, all on her own.

Perhaps she ought to have told Howie about Alexander, asked him how to deal with this ruin: What am I supposed to do now? What have I become? It turned out she did want her life to be a tragedy, just as Howie had once suggested. Now at last she truly understood: she didn't want an ordinary life. She wanted either rapture or ruin, and now there was no having either. There was no relief in this knowledge, only resignation that things would go on in this horrible way forever.

And what about Simon? And what about Red, her smallest son, her little Riddley, her dear Red, her sweet child like a baby panda? Red with his saucered eyes, his quick, easy smile, who ran to her saying "Mommy!" when she picked him up at school. Red whose small body sighed in sleep in the room above them, Red whose words came out as sweet lisps, Red who wanted to, but couldn't yet, read. Every day for a week, she and Jamie had struggled to get Red through the door at school. They would arrive for 8:20 and she would feel his body getting stiffer and stiffer, his mitten-clutch tightening. At 8:25 his eyes would well up with tears as he stood still as prey, as a deer, alert. The bell would ring and the children line up. Red would not let go of her hand. "I can't, Mommy, I can't I can't."

"You can," she told him.

She would try to walk him into the building but he would bolt, running desperately away like a man cornered by police. He knew there was no escape. She would pick him up as he thrashed. "No, I can't, I can't." The words of a woman in labour, she thought. They were her own words.

I can't I can't I can't I can't.

You can.

Oh, to have a good mother come to tell you that you could. For someone good to love you.

She had to force him. She had to force Red's body—mittens now dangling from his sleeves by strings—into the school hallway and into the teacher's arms. "He'll be okay," the teacher told Francine the first time. But Red gave her a hard look, the look of a person betrayed.

"No, Mommy! No, Mommy," he screamed as the door shut, his wail audible through the door.

When it was over, she saw the other parents watching her in pity and with judgment; she felt their eyes like heat on her face, on her neck. Someone tried to say something kind, but still her muscles ached. The tendons around her neck and shoulders ached as though torn. Also, she was crying. "You shouldn't cry in front of them," she heard someone say. "Shouldn't cry in front of children."

"Kids go through things," Jamie said, to comfort her. But his comfort was also condemnation. And so was Red's fear.

SHE AND JAMIE hired a babysitter and went for a long walk through the village together, with the idea that they would stop for a movie along the way. But even as they walked, the scandal-loving part of her hoped that Alexander would appear on the street, and see them. She knew how monstrous this was, how odious—she still wanted Alex for herself, she wanted him to be heartbroken and jealous.

"Let's drive to another cinema," she said to Jamie. "We're too close to home here." The village cinema, old-timey and quaint, was next to Café Augusta. Her parents lived nearby, too, and her brother. "Remember when we said we'd leave this stupid city when I finished my Ph.D.?"

Jamie nodded. They backtracked and got into their car, strapped on their seatbelts, and Jamie turned to reverse the vehicle, his face near her face. She felt a thrill of attraction for her husband, her long-time love made strange and erotic by her affair.

"Yup. And where would we go?"

"Montreal?" she said.

"We'd go wherever you found a job."

"Or we could just go now."

"We could."

"It would be nicer than having to see Philip all the time, trying to forgive, obsessively apologizing—" she said, feeling cruelty slip into her voice.

"You shouldn't make fun," Jamie said. "He's really making an effort, I think."

"You think it's genuine?"

Philip had called her to take a first step toward making amends, and she had nervously agreed. He seemed as committed to this project as he had been to his previous "hard boundary" between them. But the fragility of this détente meant that she had not confronted him about Howie, about what he had done all those years ago to betray her.

She and Jamie drove up to a set of big-box stores that had been built when they were both high school students, and now were shabby with age. As she and Jamie walked towards a chain restaurant, crossing shiny wet asphalt reflecting lampposts in the vast parking lot, she had a sudden realization that she was okay. She and Jamie were going to be okay. She'd done a bad thing, but the punishment wouldn't be as difficult as she'd fantasized. She held on to her husband's hand like a young child holds a parent's. Why not be good to each other? What was that poem her brother used to recite? "Ah, love, let us be true / to one another." Yes, here was her pathology: she could use love and obsession as a crowbar to break open the tightly closed wooden box that she was—break it open until she was nothing but a pile of lumber. And then her husband could piece her back together. Jamie was the person to depend on.

She stood in line with Jamie, waiting for their cappuccinos. She used other people for Jamie's sake. For him! She glowed now, filled with love for him, still holding his hand like a child. Men liked you to depend on them. Men liked a ruined woman.

The restaurant was too hot, and after they paid for their coffee, she and Jamie took off their coats and scarves and faced each other across a table. They had an hour before the movie.

"You're very handsome, you know," she said.

"You're very pretty," he said.

"We could pretend to be on a first date."

"Or we could just be ourselves and that would be more fun."

"A lot of people are opening their marriages," she said.

He laughed. "What?"

The restaurant was filling with people, and the bright, bustling indoors contrasted with the growing dark outside, the threat of ice and rain. Francine's fingertips warmed on her shallow coffee mug. She wished she could have talked to Howie about everything. Even the most meagre of decisions. "I just always want—"

"You always want . . . ?"

"I think maybe what I want is to confer with everybody I love. I want more people in my life to confer with."

Jamie looked stumped at this, but willing to go along with her, to be amused. As soon as lust lost its force in a marriage, all else between spouses became mysterious, Francine thought. This is what it was to be an animal and human both. This is what it was to have a mind.

"Lately, you seem less unhappy than you've been," Jamie said.

She lifted her mug. "Do you ever see someone else in the throes of their joy and it makes you sick?"

"What? No."

"Like you've seen them having sex? I saw this person today riding a bike in the snow and she had this look on her face, this horrible grin, her face beaming. It felt awful to be invited into her rapture. We should be private about our ecstasies. Christians always forget that, too."

"To be private about their ecstasies? Yeah, maybe."

"It's upsetting to see another person overwhelmed with joy."

"That feels so dark I want to contest it," Jamie said. "But I can't think how."

"That's what I'm here for. That's why you married me. Because you like feeling how dark things are without having to be dark yourself."

"What else could marriage be for?" he said.

SEVERAL NIGHTS IN a row, Red woke up in the night screaming. Francine went to his room to hold and comfort him. When he'd been a tiny baby, she'd held him in this same three-a.m. light, the world outside silent except for the infrequent slide of tires over slush, the bedroom warm in the glow of a night light. Back then, she had sat in this same rocking chair as their bodies dipped back and up, back and up. Whose body was this, the one that kept everyone else warm?

Now Red was a kindergartner, even though he was still her baby. Comforting him would be a kind of atonement. A bad woman could make herself good by the red blush of her son's ladybug lamp. A bad woman could make herself good by shushing her child, by putting her body in exactly this spot.

Often, she'd fall asleep in Red's bed. But deep in the night, she too would wake up, afraid of that thing she'd felt rushing at her in the coffee shop. She and Howie—both had acted with that innocent charisma of King David. You could abuse your power without knowing it.

28

PHILIP, PRESENT.

Philip was sitting in his car, waiting and watching. Despite what he'd promised Kristal he hadn't been able to resist driving past Francine's house some mornings; on those mornings, if he saw his sister leave her home, he'd resisted the urge to follow. But today he'd watched her pace quicken, watched her look guiltily over her shoulder before opening the door of her old Toyota. Heart pounding, he'd slipped his car into the lane behind hers, watched her weave erratically through the streets. It felt eerily like the time he'd trailed her to Perth; he remembered how grimly determined and glowering he'd been behind the wheel. And there she was now—his sister—outside an old coffee shop, embracing Howie, her coat wrapping around them both as though no time had passed.

Now he had a decision to make. It was a cold January day,

and he had to pick up his daughter from her day program, and he didn't have much time to sit there deciding. Howie looked less in command of himself than Philip had remembered. Howie was just a man and therefore frail; he had no particular wisdom. As a child Philip had trusted him, and he'd been fooled. Back then, he had needed this seemingly exemplary man to tell him what morality was, what adulthood was, what a man could be. He had needed the man's apparent goodness and his strength. Philip's mother was mean—might as well admit it. And his father was a person deflated by the meanness of his spouse. Philip had deliberately chosen a spouse totally different from his mother and had therefore changed at least that part of the marital pattern—but he'd still yearned to be like Howie, or something like he imagined Howie to be. A person who found it easy to be kind, easy to share happiness with others. But now here was an older Howie, wearing a cheap blue parka that was tearing at the elbows, little childish nubs at the end of fraying strings hanging out of its hood.

Francine still loved Howie, and Philip could see that too. He could see she too was frail, alone and vulnerable, wearing a face of pure need and pure desire that she never wore when he was around. This, he saw, was her private face. Philip realized with surprise that he pitied his sister. How sad it was, that she and Howie had been carrying some sort of flame for each other all these years. He wondered how they had reconnected. The last time he'd checked, Howie was living in Alberta and hardly traceable on the internet. Howie had fled Perth before any consequence could level him, before anything more than a rumour could come to light, and for a long time, Philip had considered it his duty to keep tabs on the man. But it had been several years since he'd checked, and perhaps Howie had come back to this area. He wondered why Howie and Francine had decided to meet here, at this place. He watched their cars leave in different directions and resigned himself: he would not keep following his sister, not keep spying. It was too sad.

Philip hated all parking lots, all cars, all generators of exhaust fumes, all pipelines. He hated the way snow turned to black-grey mush. After Francine's car had disappeared from view, he went into the coffee shop. It had been well preserved, and did not have the renovating upgrades of most of the other shops that were part of this chain. He went in and ordered an old-fashioned glazed and a double-double and sat for a minute, as though he actually were a detective. Again, though, it was all too sad: there was absolutely no thrill in it.

This was his decision, then: he would end this nonsense, this loop, now. He would be an adult and a decent person. He would stop making this tangled sorrow about himself.

He finished his donut and drove home, filled with purpose and with love, love he showered on Celine when he picked her up, love he bestowed on Kristal when she arrived home to a house filled with the aroma of an elaborate meal. He had made their favourite vegan stew with chickpeas and curry powder and cauliflower and sweet potatoes. This would be a relief, this love and mercy, if he could hold on to it. He read Celine more books than usual that night, and lay with her until she fell asleep—beautiful, angelic, with a hand loosely resting on his shoulder.

When Kristal mentioned how happy he seemed, he said, like a promise: "It's over. I feel sorry for my sister. I don't feel angry anymore, I feel sorry."

That night, he and Kristal made each other come, and he felt filled with gratitude for his wife's beauty, her tumble of hair, her intelligent eyes, the soft flesh of her arms and legs. He liked to smoosh her body up as though she had no skeleton. "I used to be so afraid of sin," he said, kissing her fingertips afterwards, kissing each one. "I'm done wasting my life now."

The next day, filled with this magnanimity, he called Francine. "I want to have you and Jamie over for a meal. I want to repair our relationship."

His sister was silent for a while on the other end of the phone. "Okay," she said at last. "Me too."

"I want to forgive you and for you to forgive me. I know I was wrong, the way I hounded you and wouldn't let up. I was wrong, and I want my sister back."

Again, there was a long silence. "Okay," she said again.

She was suspicious. She was skeptical. That was okay. There was time to convince her that it would be all right. They had a good lifetime ahead of them to be close again. There was lots of time.

A CLOSING

. . . so difficult is it to grasp this
advent of nothingness and to resign
ourselves to believe in it.

—GUSTAVE FLAUBERT, *Madame Bovary*

∞

FRANCINE, PRESENT.

"**Y**our mother's on the phone from the cottage," Jamie said. "She wants us to pick up mayonnaise and horseradish."

"Why doesn't she just go into town?"

Jamie stood in the door frame of the main-floor bedroom. Francine was beside the bed, packing her bag. She pulled the zipper up and around and looked at him. He shrugged, phone in hand. "She says she's got a lot to do around the house?"

"Of course," Francine said. "No problem."

"Mommy, Mommy, Mommy!" Red screamed from the top of the stairs. "Mommy, how many doggies can I bring?"

"Bring them all," Francine said, ducking out to look at him. He was clutching at least seven stuffed animals in his small arms. She caught a glimpse of her face in the mirror over her dresser and looked quickly away. It was only a year since she'd gone to the cottage with Alexander. And it was six years since the whole family had been there for their catastrophic argument. Now here they were, gathering again. It was just the sort of people they were.

Francine's hands trembled as she folded her sons' pajama pants. She had not pleaded illness or said that it was not a good idea, even though she was afraid of how she would feel in the car, travelling those familiar roads. Even though she was always the one with feelings, always the one destroyed.

But maybe she was being dramatic, she thought, when they were finally on the road. Jamie was driving and the boys were safely strapped into their seats, and they were in the van this time, not the Camry, and they were driving in daylight, and nothing about the experience felt similar to the previous time. This was not that. She was not even the same person anymore. It was possible to be more than one person in a lifetime. And that fact, she thought, might be one definition of duplicity.

"Are you worried about Philip at all?" she asked Jamie.

"We won't let anything get out of hand again." Jamie's eyes were on the road; he did not look at her.

"But hasn't he seemed a little unstable to you these past few months?"

"Well, there's something a bit unstable in his passion for this get-together. And in his obsession with forgiveness now, yeah," Jamie said.

After Philip's phone call back in the winter, suggesting that they try to forgive each other, Francine had gone over and over in her mind the scene from when she was seventeen, alone in her bedroom and weeping while Philip was on his way to Howie's to end her relationship. Sometimes when she thought about it her breath caught—she couldn't breathe, thinking about the loss of what might have been, the unknown loss, and the rage she felt that her brother had so righteously taken her life into his hands. Sometimes, though, she felt grateful to him, and this is why she had not confronted him over his betrayal. Philip had spared her that sorry road and had bolted her to some other road, a better one, the one leading here. In those moments, she felt as though some loop were closing.

The vistas outside were green and prettily rural. "The cows are lowing, Mom, look!" Simon said.

Francine and Jamie shared a smile. Simon thought that lowing was not a sound but meant that the cows were sitting down. How glad she was for her children, her husband, this life. How had she been spared a terrible reckoning? Only a year ago she had wanted to be annihilated. Had wanted—had hoped— to be destroyed. But Jamie had never let on that he suspected her of anything other than her usual distracted volatility, her routine storms and crises. If he surmised there was anything to forgive, he had already done so. She drew in a deep breath, let it out slowly.

"It's so good for the boys to have this outdoor time. To go swimming. To be with their granddad," she said.

"And Grandma!" Red squealed.

FRANCINE'S MOTHER HAD moved the dead plant off the porch, leaving behind only a round, dark mark, soil or mildew, on the concrete. The boys, unstrapped from the van, ran around the outside of the house to the tire swing hanging from the weeping willow. The tree bent toward the ground, its branches dragging into the water: a haggard old woman. Francine yelled at the boys to stay away from the corn, which was fully green now and eight feet high, while Jamie carried two suitcases into the house.

"You cut your hair again," Victoria said, receiving the grocery bag and not bothering to offer a hug or her usual cheek-kisses.

Francine put her hand up to touch the soft inch of hair on her neck. "You like it?"

Victoria would not commit to approval or disapproval. "Well. This cottage time will be good for the kids."

Jamie climbed the stairs with more bags, and Francine followed her mother into the kitchen. She waved in passing to her father, who had followed the children outside and now sat at the wooden table on the porch with an open newspaper fluttering lightly in his hands. Francine picked up a large piece of pottery and moved it to the kitchen island's granite counter.

"Just a few dollops of mayonnaise," her mother said.

Standing in the kitchen, in the exact spot where she'd been a year ago, Francine felt gratitude again. Nothing terrible had befallen her. Alexander had not recorded her or taken pictures, she had not sent him nudes, and if he had told his friends about what had happened, she hadn't had to face any repercussions. Alexander was, no doubt, finding out that the world was his. He was not like her. And it had only been that one weekend at the cottage, a few midday trysts, and then it was over and she had been slotted back into her life. He'd been eighteen last year. There could be no jail time, and there was no public shaming, no loss at all.

"Steven and Henry are due soon," her mother said, "and Philip and Kristal will be here in an hour or so, I think. Have you seen

Celine lately, my god! She's a beauty like her mother."

Victoria had begun overusing expressions such as "my god" and "Jesus Christ" years ago, around the time that Francine and Philip had started going to church. It was a subtle and unprovable way of getting under their skin.

"Don't know if I told you," she continued. "Someone broke in here last year."

Francine's hand on the wooden slotted spoon she was using, gently, to mix mayonnaise into cold macaroni, went slightly numb. "What?"

"We had a break-in. Probably just teenagers. Drank a couple of bottles of wine, knew where the key was. Didn't take anything. There was really nothing to take, of course. But nothing was broken or anything."

"That's so strange," Francine heard herself say.

"At first I felt violated. I mean, they bypassed the alarm. So we changed the security system over and we changed the locks, of course. Remind me to give you a key."

"Oh. That's okay."

"I suppose I should have asked before. But it wasn't you?" her mother said.

"What?" Francine stopped her stirring.

"It wasn't you and Jamie that came last year to use the house?"

"No. Of course not. No."

"Okay," Victoria said, her voice clipped. The boys were running after their grandfather in the yard, shrieking and finally taking him down to jump on him. "Is everything all right, Francine?"

"Everything's great," Francine said. "We're busy as ever, of course."

"You quit your job at the school."

"We were so busy. We're happier now, I think. People do change their lives, you know. And the point for me had never been to teach."

"I would hate to see you not complete your Ph.D. You have such potential."

"I don't know if 'potential' is a word that applies to a thirty-six-year-old mother of two."

"You could work for another thirty years if you chose."

Her mother was about to tell her she'd wasted her gifts, her mind, her beauty, and yes, she had in fact used *up* her mind, used *up* her beauty. Alexander on the bare mattress. Howie and his wind chimes.

Jamie came into the kitchen asking if he could help. He wore long, fitted shorts and a tight tank over his lean body—looking better, certainly, than Howie had at his age.

"Just in time," she said, unable to help the snide edge that had slipped into her voice. "There's my knight in shining armour."

FRANCINE'S FATHER HAD resisted further requests for rough-housing and gone to sit at the outdoor table. "Philip will be here soon," she said. "Dinner's almost ready."

Her father looked up from the paper and smiled at her gently, with mild incomprehension—because when anyone was arriving was of no interest to him. He had retired several years ago from work that had become so specialized it hardly made any money anymore. He liked to focus on details in his woodworking now, rather than complete new pieces. Meanwhile Victoria, now an emeritus professor, worked harder, faster and more perfectly at everything. Today she was a flurry of chicken-marinating and salad-tossing while he clutched a newspaper and was not wearing a watch.

"Have you been talking to Philip much lately?" Francine asked. "Has he mentioned how we've been getting along?"

"You'll have to ask him that," her father said vaguely.

"No, I mean we *have* been getting along better."

He squinted at the boys, now up to their ankles in the sludge of the so-called stream, and then squinted at her.

"Remember," she said, "how he thought I was so unforgivable? Last time we were here?" A door opened, and she saw herself walk through.

"I remember he was very upset."

"He certainly was very upset," she nearly growled, despite herself. She and Jamie had agreed to leave the past alone, but here she was, dredging it up. She was a machine whose buttons had been pushed. Stop it, she told herself.

She heard the hum of her mother's lovely alto, that lecturing tone she used to explain Pollock and Picasso, followed by Jamie's voice, low and laughing.

The screen door popped open and there he was, looming, surveying, a strange grimace on his face: her twin.

THE FAMILY GATHERED linens and plates, then sat down to barbecued chicken breasts and macaroni salad and some sesame-sprinkled wilted kale Francine had made that nobody else would eat.

"In the morning, we'll go for a swim," her father said.

"Yeah!" Red's chubby cheeks and white-blonde hair made him look so much like a baby that Francine felt a prick of concern.

It was a pity. He'd got the wrong mother. He had not got the good mother he deserved.

"Make sure you bring me with you," Francine said. "The boys aren't very strong swimmers yet."

Across the long table, from where he was seated near Victoria, Philip gave her a look. "I'm sure Dad can handle it."

"Are you going to accuse me of being ungrateful again? Because I'm worried about my kids?"

Jamie raised his eyebrows at her and reached around Red to cut his meat.

"This is why people get frustrated with you," said her mother, not looking up. "You always want to stir the pot."

"Like a witch? With a cauldron? People do get frustrated with me about that." Francine picked up her glass of rosé and sat back in her chair. "How powerful I can be."

"Has it been very cold down at the beach?" Jamie said to her father. "Will we need wetsuits?"

"What's a wetsuit?" said Simon.

"Wetsuits use a kind of technology," her father said. Francine saw her mother's jaw tighten while her father explained insulation to the kids.

"You do know why people get frustrated with you, Francine," Kristal offered, meekly, and Francine flashed her eyes at her sister-in-law.

"Who are these 'people'?" Francine said, bending her fingers into air quotes. "I don't want to stir the pot, you know."

"Then don't," Philip said.

"Same to you."

"Both of you cut it out," Victoria said. But to Francine it did seem as though something had possessed both her and her brother. Something in the air, in this combination of people. Something about the white tablecloth, the blue-and-white china, even the warm, shifting breeze.

"I'm trying," Francine said.

"Can we not do this in front of the kids?" Kristal said.

Red, Simon and Celine, all sitting in a row.

Francine felt a storm gathering: she felt the pressure and soon there would be tears. Her lips trembled. The children were watching her now, and Jamie made an effort to engage them in a distracting conversation about cornfields and s'mores and what it was like to be a Boy Scout.

Her mother dropped her silverware onto her plate to communicate extreme exasperation. "I'm just going to come out and say it. Your brother feels that when you went off with that youth pastor, you abandoned him. And he's felt that way ever since, despite his attempts to forgive."

"When I went *off* with?"

"Not that *we* blamed you for that. You were such an intense girl. And you spent so much time at the church. But Philip's faith meant a lot to him. Though I know it meant nothing to you."

A storm was also gathering on Philip's face. He looked at Francine expectantly.

"We didn't blame you," Victoria said again.

Her father continued chewing, as though on cud, empty-headed, passive.

"But we did think," her mother said, lowering her voice. *The cows are lowing*, Francine thought. "It was really disgusting what he did. That Pastor Howie. We were very upset to find out that he was taking advantage of you."

Francine stood up, and at the same moment she could feel movement and sound behind her, as though her standing had caused it, and then the back door flapped open. Steven came down the back steps, followed by Henry, who was small, slender, fine-featured. He held a large, attractive Bernese mountain dog loosely by a leash. The dog pulled at the tether, tail wild. "He's friendly," Henry shouted. "He just wants to say hello."

"Mom!" Red said, as Simon and Celine ran to the dog. Red's face wore an unendurable expression, the facial equivalent of a whine. He clutched Jamie.

Francine's father stood now, too, and pretended to enjoy the dog sniffing at his tube socks, while her mother exclaimed over Steven and Henry, how wonderfully well they looked. A dozen flies were hovering and landing on the food. Francine felt an insect-like casing hardening around herself.

"Francine, how are you?" Henry said, with the wealth-soaked formality her mother loved. Even now, Victoria was watching, gleaming with admiration. Why, thought Francine, were two attractive men who didn't want children more highly evolved in her mother's eyes than she was—was it because they were in deeper control of their bodies than plumping, leaking women?

"I'm dandy," she said. "And I've just heard the most astonishing news. That it's somehow my fault that when I was seventeen some thirty-year-old authority figure wanted to—" She was aware of her sons and niece in earshot, aware of how badly she was behaving. "Because somehow, no matter what happens, everything is my fault," she finished.

It was as if her words had soiled the crisp white shirt Henry was wearing. Her brother-in-law knew enough to back away from this dangling bait. But her mother did not. Her mother knew, and had taught Francine, only how to dangle or to bite.

"No one thinks that, Francine."

"It sounded to me that you thought he was taking advantage of me, but you did nothing to stop him. I remember you saying, *What did you do, Francine?*"

"I never said that. I didn't have any idea what was going on."

"You said, *I know you.* Mom, you said those exact words." Francine could barely choke out the words.

"I don't have any memory of that."

"We're not doing this," Steven said, putting an arm around Henry's waist.

"I just know how much Philip's faith meant to him," Victoria said. She looked like she had just received a hard slap. "It meant so much."

"I know you're still in touch with him," Philip said then. "With Howie."

There was a sound in Francine's ear like the gaping emptiness inside seashells, the sound everyone pretended was the ocean. Jamie dipped his head to look at her in his curious, compassionate way. "You're still in touch with Howie?" he said.

"Wait a minute," she said, turning to Philip. How smug he looked. "Are *you* in touch with Howie?" The men surrounding her, all looking ready to shake their heads and scold her. That Francine, that bad girl. "I'm not," she said to her husband. "Philip is misunderstanding something."

"Am I?"

Even the beautiful dog looked at her skeptically now.

"I need to go inside." Francine walked quickly back into the house and went to the powder room, where she bent over the toilet, hoping to vomit. Had Philip been following her again?

She wiped her mouth, though vomit had not come, and sat on the cold tiled floor staring at the toilet. Her mother *had* said, that day she went to meet Howie at Tim Hortons, *What did you do? What have you done?*

And when she had so brashly left home and travelled all that way north to find Howie? When she had come home smelling of him? What had everyone said? *What did you do? What have you done?*

Was she now a scapegoat? The idea that Jesus had died so that no human needed to be burdened by their sin seemed absurd to her, it seemed unjust. It was why she could never have truly believed in the resurrection, despite working for a decade on that scene with Mary in the garden. She didn't know what she believed. Maybe she didn't know what it *was* to believe.

She got up and went to the kitchen, where she found Philip. His face was still that of the boyish, big-eyed seven-year-old who'd follow her around saying *my favourite.* "I know you've been angry with me this whole time, despite all the talk of forgiveness," she said. "It feels like you want me not to exist."

"Come on," he said. "Honestly, I feel sorry for you."

Outside, the meal had resumed without them.

"Francine, I have to ask you, are you having an affair with someone—" Philip said. "Are you having another affair?"

"I don't know why that would be your business."

"And I know you've been in touch with Howie this whole time."

She froze. "And *that's* not true, and not your business either. Can't you leave me alone?"

"Who were you here with last summer?"

Out the window, she could see Red on Jamie's lap. They both looked tired, and there was a new expression on her husband's face, one she couldn't recognize. Shame, maybe?

"You can tell me who it was." Philip leaned against the counter with his palms braced on the granite.

"Why are you standing here?"

"I came in to check on you. To tell you . . ."

All these years they'd been each other's shadows.

"To tell me what?" Francine said.

"You know how Mom is," he said.

"Tell me what?" she repeated.

"Mom was talking just now, while you were in here, about how there was a break-in last year. And she asked Jamie if it had been you guys who'd used the cottage without permission. And Jamie said that no, it hadn't been him—"

"I already told her it wasn't us." But Francine clutched the counter. She felt like an old woman trying to hold her old sin in her hand like a fish, a dead fish, a fish cold in her hands. Who could live with this shame? Who could live, knowing there would be no absolution? For years she'd been hounded for the wrong sin, but her family wasn't wrong about her. As though determined to do so, she'd eventually proven them right.

"And I wasn't thinking, and I . . ."

"What?"

"I told them that you'd been here last year."

"That I'd been here? How did you—?"

"Sheryl texted me. I told you—remember?"

But Francine could hardly remember anything now. All she could recall were the cuffs on Alexander's pants. How thrilled he'd been. The wine gurgling darkly into one glass and then another. *The corn will be taller than you.*

She took one last glance at her beautiful husband, looking toward the house, now, right at her, looking like a man bereft, ashamed—angry, even? Looking, certainly, like a man who no longer loved her. She could not go out there to face that crowd, not even her little Red, her sweet Simon. She had to get her babies out of here, but she couldn't face them.

This house was a fever, and this family the infection. She rushed to the front door, grabbed her car keys from the hook, and hoisted herself into the van. Her hands were slick and she fumbled to put the key into the ignition. Philip came around to the window. "I'm sorry," he said, or she thought he said, through the glass.

It had rained the night previously, and the van fishtailed slightly as it found its grip on the still-slick gravel drive. She drove fast, blinded by tears, limbs heavy with adrenaline. When she reached the main road, she put her blinker on and rifled through the old CD sleeve until she found that Tragically Hip album Howie had played for her.

The world was filled with green corn and enormous, leafy trees. Her chest heaved, but she could not catch her breath. The word *scapegoat* stuck in her throat. The English word came from a misreading of a Hebrew word, which was probably the name of a demon. But a scapegoat *was* a demon, she thought. Even if it had to be innocent, too. Both were true.

In the rear-view mirror, her brother stood still as a tree, his hands on his hips. She turned right and pushed the gas pedal down. She wanted to feel her head jerk backward when she slammed on the accelerator. She would go and buy cigarettes, she thought. This is only a fever, only a dream, she thought—before the realization hit that she could not go back. She turned her head to see Red's beagle stuffy strapped into Simon's booster seat. It gazed at her with the sweetness and trust of the young and the animal, with unknowing eyes.

It didn't take long for her to lose control. She was going 100, 110, 120 on this minor road, and saw too late that the person ahead of her was braking. Through her tears she could see nearly nothing. Finally, finally, she thought, her soul might lift from her godawful body, her traitor of a body with its stupid heart, and after she slammed the brakes too late, after she'd swerved in the wrong direction, she only wished it hadn't been Philip she'd spoken to last, even if this was what she, what they both, deserved. She somehow had time to think this as an oncoming truck barrelled at her, too fast for turning. Why hadn't she sat at the table and shut her mouth? Why hadn't she been holding her child, why not hold Simon, hold Red? Her boys in the yard under the willow. The willow slowly sweeping the water with its tusks. A husband. A husband's love. A body, which could go to pieces. A body, which was only blood and bone sorted into alleyways and rooms.

Oh, she had deceived herself. Let there be a God, she thought, with surprise. It was the last thing—*my mind, my good mind*—it was the last thing she thought. Here it came, something terrible and new, and as familiar to her as her own name.

ACKNOWLEDGEMENTS

I used a few charms in the writing of this book: Baz Luhrmann's *Romeo + Juliet,* the score of which has been haunting me since the 1990s; the story of Mary Magdalene in the garden (the "Noli Me Tangere"); and Roland Barthes' *A Lover's Discourse.* My love for the work of Douglas Hofstadter, whose *I Am a Strange Loop* inspired the title, goes far beyond the affection a person should feel toward a book of philosophy.

I am so grateful to Samantha Haywood, my extraordinary agent and advocate. And to the team at Knopf Canada, including Rick Meier, one of this book's first and best readers; and Lynn Henry, whose edits deeply moved me.

I am fortunate to have many people in my life who have supported me as mentors, friends, and colleagues: thanks to Charlie Foran, Richard Bausch, Bob McGill, Joanna Levin, and Anna Leahy. To my friends Ben Pfeiffer, Alexander Lumans, Benjamin Schaefer and to all my Chapman, YDubs, Bread Loaf, and Sewanee pals. Thanks to my beloved friends Stephanie Sikma, Amanda Leduc, Tomma Velez, and Nicola Irvin. To Linda Sherman-Nurick, the most passionate bookseller. To Jack Wallis: I'm so grateful to have had your intelligence applied to my work.

It was at Tin House Summer Workshop where I began working on *Loops* in earnest: it was Aimee Bender's lecture that made me realize this was the thing I most wanted to work on, and it was in Naomi Jackson's workshop where I shared this novel's first pages. My crew there also gave me deep and lasting friendships: thanks to Sandra, Leah, Sarah, Zeyn, Emily K., Emily A., Joyce, Raad, Adrienne, and, of course, Natalie McAllister Jackson and Jaclyn Adomeit.

I need some word bigger than *gratitude* for Andreja Novakovic, my confidante and sharer in ideas, who fed me books on desire and with whom I have shared many weird and wonderful encounters. And to Seyward Goodhand, o kindred demon, o sparkling mind, o great love.

To my children, Fiona, Simone, and Juliet, who delight me and make me proud. And to Adam Harmer, and to this house we built together.

ABOUT THE AUTHOR

LIZ HARMER's first novel, *The Amateurs*, was a finalist for the Amazon First Novel Award. Her award-winning stories, essays, and poems have been published widely, and she has been a fellow at both the Bread Loaf and Sewanee Writers' Conferences. Raised in Hamilton, Ontario, she now divides her time between Southern California and Ontario.